APOCALYPSE SPRING

APOCALYPSE SPRING

Tyler H. Jolley
Holli Anderson

I dedicate this to all the cassette and VHS tapes of the '80s.

CHAPTER 1

Matt stared at his remaining friends gathered around the circular, portal-like window. It reminded him of the submarine ride at Disneyland, and he wondered briefly if the amusement park was even still standing. He'd just reentered the air-lock room after taking a short walk outside through the black, tar-like substance that covered every surface.

So much had happened in a matter of days. When Kyle had slipped from Matt's hands into the raging flash flood, it had nearly broken him. He'd never seen someone die. And it wouldn't be his last. The tall, lanky boy from Utah was the next victim. Crushed. Victoria's and Rhett's deaths marked the most gruesome demise he could have imagined. That was until what happened to Kim. He shuddered. Her melting face would haunt him for the rest of his life—which at this rate, might not be very long.

But he was proud of the last twenty-four hours. They'd made it out of that man-made hellscape, and without losing anyone else.

He set his gas mask on the padded floor. "Well? Who's with me? Who's going with me to find our families?" His gaze lingered on Catherine longer than the others. He really hoped she'd overcome her fear and come with him.

"I don't know, man." Justin gestured to the window. "This is . . . it's crazy out there."

Matt stepped closer, peering out at the raging, schizophrenic weather.

Stacy, closest to the window, started to narrate what was going on outside, completely ignoring Matt's question. "Look, it's snowing. Like, real snow, not the man-made stuff like at Camp New Beginnings." She gasped. "Is that a meteor?"

A fiery red orb with a flaming tail shot across the darkened sky, disappearing somewhere in the distant fog.

"That, little lady, is indeed a meteor," Cody said. "That's the second one I've seen since that crazy elevator dropped us off here."

Catherine shuddered at the mention of the elevator. Her face was just starting to return to its natural color after the long, nauseating ride.

Stacy continued to stare out the window. "Snow stopped. Now it's raining." The rain splattered straight down onto the ground for a minute or two, splashing into the black dirt, before there was a sudden change in direction. "The wind must be blowing, like, really hard all of a sudden. Look, the rain is falling *sideways* now!"

Darin stepped closer to her and rested his hand on the small of her back. She smiled up at him.

"We should decide what we're going to do." Catherine frowned, not taking her eyes off the ash-colored whirlwinds dancing around like miniature tornados from hell. "I don't want to stay here. It's so . . . eerie."

"Maybe we should just go back to the control room and think on it for the night," Justin said.

Stacy looked at Catherine and smirked. "You up for another hour-and-a-half ride on the *hellivator*?"

Catherine's face paled, and she wrapped an arm around her abdomen. "No. But I don't know which is worse: the elevator or this creepy room."

"It's not that creepy," Matt said, looking around at the cracked yellow padding of the walls. He pointed at one of the many panels with broken gumdrop buttons and small indicator lights, the covers of which were milky with age. He smiled. "It reminds me of the hallways in the Millennium Falcon. Or the med bay in *Alien*."

"Yeah." Cody nodded. "And you're Han Solo, and Justin is Chewbacca—because he's tall, ya know? And hairy."

"And no one understands him when he talks," Darin added with a chuckle.

Justin rolled his eyes. "You guys are real hilarious. You're just jealous of my studly physique and gorgeous locks." He ran his fingers through his sandy-blond hair, then flexed his arms so his biceps popped out.

Yeah, Matt thought as he eyed Justin's bulging muscles, *maybe just a little.*

"Besides," Justin said, "it's Texas here who no one can understand, with his Southern drawl, and 'y'alls' and 'ma'ams.'" He nudged Cody with his shoulder.

The small group laughed, which relieved some pressure from Matt's chest. That's what he'd been aiming for, to defuse some of the building tension in his friends.

The building shuddered, followed closely by a groan from deep in the earth. Catherine and Stacy screamed, and Stacy buried her face in Darin's chest. "Was that an earthquake, Lance-Darin?" The words came out muffled against his shirt.

"I . . ." His voice was a higher pitch than normal. He cleared his throat and put his arms around her. "I don't know. Maybe."

Catherine looked out the window. "Look, it's hailing out there. I've never seen hail that big before." Her voice quivered a little, and her eyes were wide as she turned to look at Matt.

He moved closer to her and put his arm around her shoulders.

"This really sucks." She swiped angrily at a tear trickling down her cheek. "The whole purpose for the cryopods and the vault and the decades-long forced sleep was so we'd miss this! So we'd wake up when this crap was all over and done with! And instead, we're stuck right smack in the middle of the apocalypse." She jerked away from Matt and scrubbed the tears from her face with both hands. "I can't watch it anymore." She staggered to the back of the air lock and slumped against the wall next to the horizontal elevator door.

They all followed her, trudging silently, mouths turned down in defeated frowns. All but Matt, who stayed by the portal window, staring out into the gloom. His thoughts turned back to his parents. He had to find them, even if he had to go it alone—but he really hoped he wouldn't have to.

A football-sized chunk of frozen ice slammed into the upper edge of the round window. Matt flinched, his heart leaping into his throat, nearly choking him. He took a deep breath and ran a hand across the short hair of his buzz cut before walking, shoulders drooping, to the back of the room to join his friends.

CHAPTER 2

Indicator lights around the room blinked off and on. Some of them were static, flickering slightly, but the light waxed and waned, like the bulb or electricity was failing. Matt slumped to the floor next to Catherine, his back resting against the cracked padding of the yellowed wall—it reminded him of the padded rooms in *One Flew Over the Cuckoo's Nest*, a '70s movie his parents rented at the local video store. Catherine sniffed and turned her face away from him, wiping again at her cheeks.

He wanted to comfort her, but he wasn't sure if her anger was directed toward him or the continuing apocalypse. He needed to bring up the idea of leaving this place again, but he didn't want to make things worse—seeing Catherine cry made his guts churn uncomfortably.

Cody saved him from having to decide. "This is as serious as a heart attack. We need to talk about our next steps. What the heck are we gonna do now?"

"First," Stacy said, "I think we should, like, list our options so we know what our choices are."

As far as Matt was concerned, there was only one choice. "Leaving what's behind us *behind us* and going to find our parents. Finding Vault B-35."

Justin rolled his eyes. "Yeah, Matt, we all know what you want to do. You haven't shut up about it."

Matt stiffened, but before he could defend his position, Catherine spoke up. "Cool it, Justin! He's just starting the list. What do *you* think we should do?"

"I don't know . . . I'd like to hear what Darin thinks. He's the only one who knows what the vault was like when we left."

Darin rubbed the back of his neck and flicked his eyes up at Justin, then down, not making eye contact with anyone. He cleared his throat. "I . . . I don't want to go to the vault. I think we should go back."

"Why?" Matt asked, frustration making his voice come out louder than he intended. "We almost died multiple times in that underground death trap! That place was falling apart around us."

"I know . . ." Darin closed his eyes and took a deep breath. "But so was the vault, last time I was there. When he woke me the second time . . . the carbon foam doesn't last forever."

"Are you talking about the meteor strike?"

Darin looked away again. "Yeah, the meteor strike." He rubbed his neck again, then wiped his hand on his pants. "It was . . . bad. It did a lot of damage. It's why your column started to fail. And like I said, the fix was only temporary, I think."

Stacy laid a hand on his arm. "It must have been awful."

"It was." He shook his head. "When the fifteen-year-olds all died . . . Westbrook . . . he lost it. He thought he'd fixed the damage, at least that's what he told me. He made me go outside with a gas mask to try to seal the cracks in the rock. But things got worse."

"So he decided to start moving us," Cody said.

Darin nodded, still not looking at anyone. "I don't want to go back there."

Matt clenched his fists. "But that's where our parents are!"

"And my brothers and sisters," Stacy whispered.

Darin looked up at her. "We don't . . . we don't even know—"

"No. We don't know," Matt interrupted. "Which is why we *have* to try to find them. We have to save them if we can." He thought of the last time he'd seen his parents. Right before they were separated to be put into suspended animation inside the cryopods. His mom's frightened tears. His dad's assurances that it was going to be okay, that they'd all be together again soon.

"I'm with Matt," Cody said. "Besides wanting to check on my folks, I *do not* want to go back down in that crumblin' cesspool."

"We don't have to go back down there," Justin argued. "We can take the elevator back to the control room, then walk, aboveground, back to the Sev."

"I love the Sev," Stacy said.

Darin continued, "We at least know it's safe there, and there's food."

"And beer," Justin added.

"But *is* it safe?" Catherine's whisper was low, and

Matt had to lean closer to hear her. "That whole area is on top of the underground 'soundstage' system. The roof was caving in on us just hours ago. The roof that is the grounds of Camp New Beginnings."

"I thought you didn't want to go out into the apocalypse, Catherine? That you were on our side." Justin nodded at Darin.

"Ugh!" Catherine growled. "I don't know what I want! Nowhere is safe."

"Exactly." Matt softened his tone and took her hand in his, worried she might pull away. But she didn't. Instead, she grasped his hand like it was a lifeline. "Nowhere is completely safe. So we should go find our parents." He looked at Stacy. "And siblings. If there's even a small chance we can save them, we need to try."

"Welp, you already know I agree with Matt," Cody said. "So how do we decide?"

"Maybe we should just go our separate ways." Justin crossed his arms and scowled.

"No," Cody said. "We need to stick together. It took all y'all to save me from the stinkin' reservoir. And Darin—no way just one of us could have pulled him out of the swirling water down there."

"What should we do, Matt?" Stacy asked. "Like, how do we decide?"

Matt's stomach twisted into a knot. He looked around, racking his brain for an idea. His gaze landed on Darin, nervously picking at a small rip in the padded wall, pulling on some thick threads dangling from the edge of the tear.

Matt sat up straighter. "Everyone pick a thread from

one of the tears in the padded walls. Only one thread each. We'll pull them out at the same time. The person with the longest thread will decide where we go."

Catherine nodded. "Like drawing straws."

"Exactly. When everyone has a hold of a thread, let me know."

When all six of them had chosen their threads, Matt said, "Okay. Pull on three. One, two, three." He winced at the short strand he now held pinched between his thumb and index finger.

The friends compared.

"Stacy wins," Matt announced, trying not to sound disappointed. She would for sure choose what "Lance-Darin" wanted.

CHAPTER 3

Darin grinned, his eyes sparkling as he looked at Stacy. But she avoided his gaze, instead staring at the six strings lying side-by-side on the dirty tile floor. She twisted her mouth, biting on her bottom lip.

Stacy exhaled loudly, then looked up at Darin, touching a hand to his chest. Her eyes glistened with newly formed tears, not yet fallen, and her voice quivered a little as she looked around the circle of friends. "Lance-Darin, I'm sorry, but . . . I think Matt's right. We need to move forward. I want to see my family too."

Darin's shoulders slumped and Justin scowled. But neither of them voiced an argument to her decision.

Releasing the breath he'd been holding, Matt's head spun a little from lack of oxygen. *Glad I wasn't standing up*, he thought. "Okay. When do we leave?"

"No time like the present," Cody said.

Stacy nodded. "Like, I don't know about you guys, but this place is so totally not rad. I agree that we should leave now."

"Yeah," Catherine said. "We slept good last night, and it's still pretty early in the day. I definitely do not want to spend the night in this creepy air lock anymore."

"Darin? Justin?" Matt forced himself to get their input even though every nerve and muscle in his body screamed to get moving.

Darin nodded. "Yeah, okay, but what about your foot?" He turned to Stacy.

Gritting her teeth and wincing, she slowly pulled her shoe off. They all looked at the damage. "I'll be okay," she said.

"We can change the wrapping before we go," Matt said.

Stacy nodded and tugged at the corner of a piece of athletic tape holding the gauze on. She winced as she freed the bandage completely and replaced it.

"Justin?" Matt asked.

"Whatever," Justin said. He pushed himself up from the floor and walked over to the small window. "Now's as good a time as ever—looks like the weather has calmed down for a minute."

They grabbed their backpacks, full of the supplies they'd collected from the control room, and gathered near the door. "Make sure our gas masks fit good before we open this door," Darin said. "The air's toxic out there."

Having been outside, brief as it was, Matt had to agree. He was glad Darin had insisted they bring them when they'd found the stash in the barracks of the control room.

Everyone fitted the full-faced masks over their heads. Darin helped Stacy by holding her strawberry-blonde hair out of the way so the mask would get a good seal, then he tightened the straps on the back of her head before putting his own mask on. Matt turned to see if Catherine needed help with her hair, too, but her dark curls were pulled back into a ponytail, and she was already pulling the straps taut on the mask.

Matt tightened his, then took a couple of deep breaths in and out to make sure the seal was good. "Ready?" He spoke loudly to be understood through the sound-muffling apparatus.

The others nodded, and Justin, who stood closest to the door, pushed it open with a whoosh. They were met with a blast of snow that immediately melted with a wave of hot air that washed over them.

Catherine grabbed Matt's hand in a death grip. Her eyes were wide and her chest rose and fell at a too-rapid rate. He smiled, squeezed her hand, and laced his fingers through hers. "It's going to be okay."

She nodded, and they ventured into the raging apocalypse.

"Which way, fearless leader?" Cody yelled.

Matt's racing heart and sudden cold sweats belied the "fearless" part as massive lightning strikes lit up the ashen sky nearby. He pointed to a foggy mountain range in the distance—to the east, he thought.

"Look at that," Cody said, gesturing.

The small group stood within a stone's throw to a narrow asphalt road. Or what was left of it. The broken blacktop had pieces of it rising up like it had boiled from intense heat. Cracks and fissures spiderwebbed throughout, parts of the asphalt fractured into dozens of smaller pieces.

"Let's follow this . . . road." Matt shrugged. "Or what's left of it."

Stepping past the group with Catherine in tow, he led the way, walking down the middle, halfway between two faded yellow lines on each shoulder of the road. There was no way two average-sized vehicles could pass each other going in opposite directions—and the absence of a middle line agreed with his assessment. The surrounding land was desolate and sandy, with outcroppings of pock-marked lava rock sticking up all over.

The wind kicked up, bringing with it frigid temperatures. Matt hunched his shoulders and dipped his head to try to block the freezing air from penetrating the bare skin of his arms. Catherine pulled her hand out of his, to his dismay, and crossed her arms over her chest, pinning her hands in the warmth of her armpits. Dark clouds rolled in with the speed of a bullet train, obscuring the red sun as it feebly tried to shine through.

Gooseflesh popped up on Matt's arms, and he wondered if it would be worth it to get a blanket out of his pack. Lightning streaked from the dark clouds, hitting the ground so close to them that the boom of thunder came almost simultaneously, rattling their eardrums. Catherine screamed, as did at least one person behind them, probably Stacy.

Catherine stepped closer to Matt, her shoulder rubbing against his, and pointed with a trembling finger at scorch marks on the ground all around them. "That's from lightning, isn't it?" Her hysterical voice barely carried through the powerful wind.

Matt nodded and pulled her to him in a one-armed hug.

"This is too dangerous!" Catherine looked behind them at the others, then at the barely visible building they'd left behind.

Matt's gaze followed hers back even as his feet continued to plod forward on the fractured road. *Maybe we should go back.* The thought ripped a hole in his chest and he faced forward again, toward the mountain he could no longer see in the distance. He couldn't abandon his parents. He *knew* they were there, and they needed his help.

Lightning pounded into the road ahead of them like Thor's hammer. Catherine screamed again and buried her head in Matt's chest, trembling sobs rippling through her body.

CHAPTER 4

As if the last bolt of electricity had hit a switch, the wind stopped, and the lightning strikes moved farther away until they could no longer hear the accompanying thunder.

Darin rushed up to Matt, Stacy hanging on to his arm as tears streaked down her face beneath the clear cover of her mask. "This is crazy, Matt!" he said. "It's too dangerous, we need to go back!"

Steam rose from the ground as the stifling heat returned. Matt readied himself for an argument, even though he knew Darin was right.

"Hey!" Cody yelled. "Look at this." He'd passed them as they prepared to face off and stood a couple of feet to the side of the pavement, his shoes almost swallowed up in the black sand.

Justin reached him first. "What the hell?"

Catherine straightened up and sniffed as she adjusted her gas mask. She, Matt, Darin, and Stacy joined Cody and Justin as they stared down at the ground.

Justin kicked at something in the sand. "It's hard, like glass."

Cody bent down and touched the rough surface of the tube-like object, the same color as the ash-stained sand surrounding it. "It *is* glass, sort of."

Catherine leaned in closer. "The lightning caused it. Intense heat turns sand into glass. It's called fulgurite, I think."

"How do you know that, genius?" Justin teased.

"My mom." Her voice hitched, and she swallowed and started again. "My mom and I took a girls' trip to Palm Springs over spring break when I was thirteen. They sell it in a lot of the little tourist shops there."

"They're all over here," Stacy said as she pointed out several within twenty yards of them. Her eyes were wide when she turned to look at Matt. "Wait . . . that means there's a lot of lightning strikes out here."

"Which is one of the many reasons why we should give up on this crazy expedition and go back to where we know we're safe. Relatively," Darin said.

Matt's stomach dropped. Darin was right; they were sitting ducks out here. Matt bent over, resting his hands on his knees as the world spun around him. "I can't—" He closed his eyes and fell back on his butt, hiding his head in his arms, folded on top of his bent knees. He barely registered the gas mask digging into his forehead. He started counting slowly—Matt-itation, his mom had called the familiar exercise—to try to stop the anxiety building in his chest.

"Matt! What's wrong?" Catherine crouched on the ground right next to him.

He hadn't even noticed her arm wrapped around his back until she spoke.

"Are you okay?"

"Give me a minute," he choked out.

She rubbed his back while he silently finished counting to ten, then back down to one. He took a deep breath and raised his head, staring out into the distance. "I can't give up on them," he whispered. "*We* can't give up on them."

"I know." She squeezed his shoulders. "But we need to find a better, safer way to get there."

Matt pushed himself to his feet and faced his friends. "You guys head back to the air lock. I'm going to keep going a little farther. You know, try to scout some things out. Maybe it gets better up ahead."

Catherine tried to hold him there, but he shrugged her off and started walking back to the road.

"Matt, buddy." Cody caught up to him in a couple of steps. "You know this is crazy, right? It ain't gonna get better up ahead. It's the apocalypse. It's the whole world."

He did know. He knew, but he didn't care. "I have to try."

They stepped back onto the pavement, and Matt's gait picked up speed. He narrowed his eyes—the road looked different a little ways in the distance. He started jogging, leaving Cody to catch up or go back, he didn't care which. Matt skidded to a stop, his toes inches from the lip of a large, ragged-edged hole in the asphalt. He dropped to his knees and peered into the opening.

He yelled over his shoulder, "Hey, guys! Get over here! I think I found a better way!"

CHAPTER 5

The road looked like it had been blasted apart where Matt stood—like a meteor had struck there, or lava had melted the asphalt and underlying ground away. He smiled. A slightly unhinged-sounding laugh bubbled up into his throat.

"There's a tunnel down here!" he yelled.

A tunnel ran directly under the road as far as Matt could see. He dropped his backpack and knelt down to unzip it as Cody, and then the rest of the group, made their way to him.

"Holy cow patties," Cody said as he came to a halt at Matt's side.

Matt pulled a flashlight from his pack and cranked the handle to energize it before shining it down into the pit. Just as he'd hoped, the beam landed on a damaged concrete walkway running parallel to the road about ten or fifteen feet down. "What do you think?" he asked Cody.

"It'll get us out of the weather."

"Well, let's get down there before the lightning, or

something worse, starts up again," Catherine said from behind Matt.

He looked up at her, smiling, and nodded. He shoved the flashlight into a side pocket of his backpack so he could reach it easily once they were in the tunnel. He stood and, in an act of spontaneous relief, hugged Catherine, the sides of their gas masks clinking together. He was glad when she hugged him back, and flooded with warmth when she squeezed harder before releasing her embrace.

"Okay, it looks like we can just climb down that pile of rubble. We'll have to hang from the edge to reach it with our feet. We can use the rope as a safety harness." Matt pulled it out of his bag and worked on tying a rope harness like he'd learned to do in Scouts. "Justin, since you're the tallest, you go first so you can reach up and help the girls if they need you to."

Justin nodded.

"Then Darin, you go next for the same reason—the two tallest at the bottom to give the rest of us a hand." Matt was no shrimp at six foot one, but Justin and Darin were taller. "Cody and I will hold on to the rope up here, since there's nothing to tie it to. The girls can go next, then Cody, and I'll climb down last."

"Sounds like a good plan," Cody said. "And at least it isn't a hundred-foot drop like the last thing we climbed down into. This'll be easy compared to that."

"Cody!" Stacy slapped him on the shoulder. "Don't jinx us!"

Justin waved Matt off when he offered him the rope harness. "Nah, chief," he said, finding a good place for a handhold. "I'll be good."

Matt watched him tug on a horizontal piece of rebar where the asphalt wasn't crumbling as much. He swung himself down feet first, hanging on with his fingers. He did a couple of chin-ups for good measure, his large biceps bulging. "That was for you, girls!" he yelled as he dropped down after the second chin-up. He easily found footing on the rubble and scrambled the last eight or nine feet down to the pathway.

Catherine rolled her eyes, and Stacy clapped at his bigheaded display of strength.

Darin, not to be outdone by Justin, refused the safety harness too. He swung down and then pulled himself up like Justin had, only his fingers slipped on the rebar, and he lost his grip with one hand.

"Lance-Darin!" Stacy yelled, clambering to her knees to look into the hole.

"I'm fine," he shouted up. His feet rested on the top of the pile, and he let go of the lip completely. It took him a little longer than Justin to climb down to the bottom; a couple of curse words broke free from his mouth as he slid the last few feet to the ground.

"All right, Stacy is coming down next." Matt helped her get into the makeshift safety harness. "Hold on to the rope with one hand, or you might tip upside down," he warned.

Stacy nodded, mouth set in a determined line. She lay down on her stomach on the cracked pavement and scooted backward until her legs dangled over the edge. She took a deep breath and looked back into the hole. "Lance-Darin, don't let me fall!"

"Never!" he replied.

The rope rested against her chest and to the side of her face. Matt and Cody pulled it tight and braced themselves to lower her down. Stacy let out a little squeak as she lost contact with the road, but the rope harness held her firm. They lowered her down to the rubble heap, then kept the rope taut as she climbed her way down into Darin's waiting arms.

The process was repeated with Catherine—except Justin helped her the rest of the way down.

"You next, Cody." Matt held out the loops of the rope harness. "I'll keep you steady as you descend."

Cody looked unsure. "I don't know, Matt. I'm pretty solid. I weigh more than I look."

"No kidding, dude. Your shoulders are as broad as a prize bull's. I'm not going to try to lower you down like we did the girls. You'll have to hang from the edge and drop to the heap. I'll just keep the rope tight so you don't go tumbling all the way down."

"I used to think five ten was an okay height . . . until I met all you six-foot-plus giants," Cody grumbled.

Matt wasn't worried. He figured Cody could probably out-bench all of them, including jock Justin.

Cody's descent went smoothly, and Matt pulled the rope back up and coiled it before returning it to his backpack. He scraped his arm on the edge of the road as he lowered himself into the hole, but other than that, it seemed like it would be an easy climb down. And it would have been if something hard hadn't sailed past his head and splattered up chunks of rubble at his legs.

CHAPTER 6

Matt hurried the rest of the way while working to avoid being hit. Golf ball-sized hail pounded through the opening, bouncing off the pile of debris. The group of teens skirted down the pathway away from the onslaught, in the direction they'd been traveling above.

"Looks like you found this tunnel just in time, Matt," Catherine said.

"Yeah." He looked back. "Getting pelted by those giant ice balls would not have been good."

Cody took his gas mask off and drew in a breath.

"What are you doing?!" Darin asked.

"Don't worry, it's fine," Cody said. "The air up there is bad because of the ash blowing around as thick as flies on a pile of manure, but down here it's pretty clean."

All but Darin took off their masks.

Catherine used the bottom of her T-shirt to wipe her face. Matt nearly choked on his own spit at the sight of her bare midriff. "I don't recommend crying while wearing a full-faced gas mask," she said.

"Totally," Stacy agreed.

The pathway looked like an extra-wide sidewalk—one that had been attacked by an army of rogue jackhammers in spots. Matt peered down the dim tunnel, grateful to realize that enough light filtered through the broken spots above that they wouldn't have to use the hand-cranked flashlights much.

As the others stowed their gas masks in their packs, Darin examined them, his face drawn tight with concern. Stacy sidled up to him and trailed a finger down the bare skin of his arm. "Lance-Darin, take that mask off so I can kiss you."

His face turned red as he glanced up at the others, then down at Stacy. Her pouty lips must have convinced him. He slowly loosened the straps around his head, then held his breath as he peeled the mask off.

"Don't be a chicken," Justin said. "Take a breath." He stepped forward and punched Darin in the gut—not hard, just with enough oomph to force him to take a breath.

Darin sucked in a lungful of the stale air and moved to shove Justin, who easily dodged out of his reach. Stacy hopped between them like a skilled cheerleader and turned Darin's face to her with a hand to each cheek. "Kiss, Lance-Darin," she reminded him.

Catherine rolled her eyes. "Uhh, we'll leave you two alone."

"But not too long," Matt said. "We aren't going to wait for you. You'll have to catch up." As they walked down the path, dodging the more jagged pieces of concrete, he wondered if Catherine might want some time alone with him . . .

Her arm brushed against his as they walked, and he smiled down at her. "Feeling better?"

She nodded. "Yeah. Sorry I freaked out a little. I'd ask if you're feeling better, but I can see that you are by the bounce in your step."

Matt laughed. "I prefer to call it a swagger. 'Bounce' sounds too bunny-like."

The swagger may have briefly turned to a bounce when Catherine slipped her hand in his, interlacing their fingers. She sighed. "I do feel a lot safer down here."

They were able to walk four abreast on the walkway, and Cody wondered aloud, "What do y'all s'pose this was built for? I mean, it's bigger than a sidewalk, but not wide enough to be a road. There aren't any tram tracks or anything."

Stacy spoke up from behind them. "It reminds me of, like, the path for a golf cart. It's about the same width, except that most of those are made out of asphalt."

"Glad you two could join us," Justin said. "You didn't spend much time playing tonsil tag."

"Ooh, barf!" Stacy said. "That makes it sound gross."

"If it's gross, then you're doing it wrong."

Darin stiffened. "She didn't say it was gross. She said the way you described it is gross."

"Relax, dude. I'm just joking."

Cody looked up through a hole big enough to see out of. "Looks like it stopped hailing."

"Way to change the subject," Catherine whispered as she followed his gaze.

"It's a gift." He shrugged.

They walked on for about an hour, occasionally having to dodge rubble that had fallen from above or what looked like hardened lava that had seeped into the tunnel. The path ahead brightened more than at their starting point, and as they got closer, it became hard to breathe. Ash swirled in the light from above. Catherine coughed and pulled her shirt collar up over her mouth and nose.

"Time to put the masks back on," Darin said, being the only adult in the group.

Stacy sighed, but they all stopped to put them on before moving closer to the area.

Matt inspected the large cave-in. Dirt, asphalt, and cement blocked the whole tunnel. "What do you think did this?"

"My guess would be a meteor," Darin said, his face turning pale.

"Yeah," Matt agreed, "that seems about right. This hole is huge. And look at the scorch marks."

"We're gonna have to go topside again," Cody said. "At least until we find another spot to climb down."

Catherine stared up into the red sky and hugged her arms around her chest. "At least there isn't lightning at the moment." She turned wide, fearful eyes to Matt.

He touched her arm. "It'll be okay. We'll get past this blockage and find another way down in no time."

"I hope so." She turned and climbed up out of the tunnel, Matt close behind her, no rope needed this time. Twisted rebar stuck out from the walls, and they used it like a warped ladder to reach the surface.

Matt was glad to see that his theory was correct: The underground tunnel followed right beneath the road.

The landscape hadn't changed much, except for the increased number of pits in the earth from falling meteors. Catherine bit her lip and looked up. "Let's hurry and find a way back in before the world decides to attack us again."

CHAPTER 7

A light wind swirled around them, kicking up the ash and dust. The air was cool, but not cold enough to be uncomfortable—at the moment. Matt searched the ground ahead of them, walking at a fast pace, determined to find a way back down to the tunnel before something else fell from the sky. He looked back at Catherine. She seemed to be doing okay, other than her eyes darting back and forth, up and down, as she watched for something ominous to occur.

The wind picked up, blowing straight at them, the temperature turning icy. The ash blowing in his face made it hard for Matt to see more than a few steps ahead, so he slowed his pace. He didn't want to fall into an open pit.

Matt breathed a sigh of relief, fogging up his mask, when he stepped to the edge of another hole big enough to climb back down into the tunnel. He turned to Catherine, who was only steps behind him. "We can go down here. It looks like less of a decline than the first one. I'm going to go down first to make sure. I'll yell up to you if it's safe."

Catherine nodded, hugging herself as she shivered. She twisted to relay the message to the others as they caught up in a group.

The hill of debris was situated almost like someone had intentionally used it to lay stairs in that spot. Even so, Matt stepped carefully in the dim light; he didn't want to twist an ankle with a misstep. He stepped onto the concrete pathway and hollered up to the others, "This one's easy, just watch your step."

Catherine started down first and took Matt's proffered hand as he helped her down the last few steps. When the group was all assembled, they walked away from the breach in the tunnel and removed their masks as soon as the air cleared.

"It would really have been nice if we would have known to wear layers for this ever-changing weather." Catherine rubbed her bare arms as they walked.

"For sure," Stacy agreed.

Catherine removed the elastic from her hair and shook it out before pulling it all back into a tight ponytail again. "I really need a shower. A *warm* shower, with clean water—not an apocalyptic rain shower full of ash and radioactive dust."

Matt looked down at his own black-streaked clothing and skin. "Yeah. We could all use a good spray down."

"Yep, you all smell like someone's gym shorts," Justin said as he jogged ahead of them.

"Well, you smell like gym shorts rolled in chicken crap," Cody yelled after him. "Chicken crap is the most foul-smelling of all the smells on a farm," he explained with a grin.

"Really?" Darin asked. "Why is that? I would think that pigs would be the worst."

Cody shook his head. "Pigs get a bad rap; they aren't nearly as smelly as chickens. Chicken poop stinks because it's high in ammonia. It's real bad when it gets wet."

They stopped and looked up to where Justin's lower body dangled from an opening in the ceiling, just big enough to fit his head and shoulders through. He dropped back down to the short pile of rubble he'd climbed up on to reach the hole. He jumped down to the pathway and shook the ash out of his sandy-blond hair.

"What were you doing up there?" Stacy asked.

"Just looking around. I kinda want to know if anything changes out there."

Stacy wrinkled up her face. "Like what? We already know that, like, the weather changes all the time."

Justin shrugged. "More like if the terrain changes or something. I don't know. Or if there's a bigfoot or aliens or something out there."

"As if." Stacy rolled her eyes.

"I used to think bigfoot was real," Darin confessed with a self-deprecating smile.

"Oh, Lance-Darin! That's so cute!"

"And who says aliens aren't real?" Matt chimed in. "What about Area 51?"

"You believe those conspiracy theories?" Catherine bumped him with her shoulder and smirked.

Matt smiled. "I believe in the possibility of those conspiracy theories."

"I had a neighbor who swore he was abducted by aliens in nineteen eighty-two," Cody said. "But then again, he also said his sheep talked to him and that he could predict the future by examining patterns in cow manure."

They all laughed as they continued along the pathway. Now that Justin had done it, they all took turns peeking out of any of the breaches in the ceiling that were big enough to poke a head through—at least for the ones that had rubble to climb up.

Matt figured they'd walked several miles, maybe more. The sore muscles in his legs told him probably more. He reached the next ceiling hole before the others, but there wasn't much of a pile to climb up on. "Hey, Justin, give me a boost."

Justin held his hands, fingers laced together, at Matt's knees. He put his foot in Justin's hands and Justin lifted him to where he could reach the edge with his own hands. Matt pulled himself up through the hole until his chest lay against the side. He held his breath as he looked around. The wind had died down and the sun was making a rare, though muted, appearance. Matt almost gasped, but remembered in time that he shouldn't breathe in the contaminated air. In the distance, through the haze, was a building. The first they'd seen since leaving the air lock.

CHAPTER 8

"Help me back down," Matt yelled when his head and torso were back inside the tunnel. He hung by his fingers, a little too far for him to just let go and drop to the pavement below. Justin wrapped his hands around Matt's right calf, and another pair of hands grasped his left calf. They lowered him down by walking their hands up his legs until his butt landed on one each of their shoulders. He wobbled and used their heads to hold on to for balance, then he dropped to the ground.

Stacy laughed. "You guys could totally be cheerleaders. Not."

"Guys." Matt ignored her jab. "I saw a building! It's in the direction we're heading."

Five questions came at him at once.

"What kind of building?"

"How far away?"

"Did it look occupied?"

"Is it damaged?"

"Do you think there's food there? Or beer?" That one, of course, was Justin.

Matt held up his hands, palms forward. "Whoa, whoa. One at a time. It was really too far away to see much, other than it looks to be a ways away and it's a few stories tall."

"Now that Justin mentioned food, I'm hungry," Cody said as the group moved away from the opening.

"Now's as good a time as any to stop and eat," Matt said.

They dropped their packs on the dusty floor of the tunnel and dug out some of the dried food they'd scavenged from the control room before beginning the ridiculously long elevator ride to the air lock.

"Who has the can opener?" Justin asked, holding up a can of peaches.

"Here." Stacy handed it to him.

"So, seriously," Catherine said, "what do you all think the building is? Best guess."

They discussed as they ate, sitting on the dirty cement, backs against the tunnel walls.

"Did you guys see *Day of the Dead*?" Matt asked. "Maybe it's a house full of zombies."

"Not funny, Matt!" Stacy shrieked.

"Yeah, man." Justin scowled. "We have no idea how the apocalypse affected people who weren't in cryopods! Don't say stuff like that!"

"Okay, okay! I was just joking," Matt said.

"I hope it's a shopping center." Stacy's eyes grew glassy.

"Seriously?" Justin snorted. "Just what we need—

makeup and perfume. Maybe some accessories for our fancy clothes." He waved his hands around his ears like a jewelry model.

"Rude! You know we could all use some different clothes. Like, at least a rain jacket or something."

"As much as I'd like it to be a store—full of food *and* clothes—I think that's really unlikely," Catherine said. "Why would something like that be here? I mean, so far, everything has been centered around the cryo experiment and prepping for the apocalypse. It's not like this is some sort of destination resort."

Cody shoved the wrapper from his dried fruit into his backpack. "Maybe it's just another control building or something. Hopefully it's like the Sev, though—a place where we can get some food and rest."

"And beer," Justin added.

"What do you think it is, Darin?" Matt asked.

He shrugged. "I have no idea. Probably an empty, bombed-out shell."

"Way to be a downer, dude." Justin gulped water from his canteen.

"Well, no matter what kind of building it is, I think we should try to make it there before nightfall." Matt stood and positioned his backpack straps across his shoulders, signaling the others that it was time to get moving again.

They walked in silence for a while. Matt watched for another place where he could peek outside again. He was pretty sure the road and tunnel would take them right past the building, but he wanted to confirm that with his vision. Plus, as they got closer, he was hoping to get some idea of what the building was and if it would be a good place to shelter for the night.

Stacy broke the silence. "So, umm, like, do you really think there might be zombies out there, Matt?"

He laughed. "No way. Zombies are just fiction. The reanimation of a corpse is biologically impossible."

"Maybe that is impossible," Justin chimed in. "But there are other things that can turn living people into brainless monsters."

"Like what?" Catherine asked.

"Like drugs that make you mental. Or diseases, brain infections that mess with your personality. Maybe radiation." Justin's voice rose in pitch with each theory.

"You forgot to mention alien probes inserted into your brain," Cody joked.

Matt laughed. "Yeah, by way of your anus."

"This isn't funny, Matt!" Stacy's eyes bulged. She was well on her way to hysteria. "You're the one who told us that aliens are real!"

"Relax, Stacy. I said that I think it's *possible* that they exist, not that they *do* exist."

Her chin trembled and her voice wavered. "But . . . what if there's something like that in that building?" She stopped, her body going rigid. "What if there's something like that down here?!"

"Shit, Stacy," Justin said. "Now you have me freaking out."

Darin put an arm around Stacy. She buried her head in his chest, and he urged her forward, guiding her down the path.

"Don't worry, little lady," Cody said. "Me and Matt

will check it out before you all go in. We'll make sure it's safe."

"And what are you two going to do?" Justin's voice rose. "Lull them to sleep talking about stupid movies and your idiot theories?"

"Whoa, Justin, not cool," Catherine said. "I don't know why you two are so worked up about this, but being a jerk isn't going to help anything."

Before he could respond, a large segment of the ceiling fell from above, bringing with it a rush of dirt, ash, and asphalt. Matt and Catherine were knocked to the side in a plume of fine dust, barely avoiding getting smashed in the head. Cody skidded to a stop and covered his face with his arms as the chunk of cement landed just inches from the toes of his shoes and burst, fragments and dust flying everywhere. Stacy screamed. Within moments, it was all over.

Matt coughed. "Everybody okay?!"

Catherine dusted herself off and helped him up.

"Yeah," Cody answered.

"We're okay," Stacy said through sobs.

"Justin?" Matt asked.

There was no answer.

Matt rushed to the center of the tunnel. Chunks of asphalt and dirt formed a new obstacle.

"Justin?!" Stacy screamed. "Justin, where are you?"

Matt's heart pounded in his rib cage, and it was hard to swallow. He knelt down and looked under the bigger chunks of road.

"Justin!" Catherine yelled. "Can you hear us?"

The teenage jock emerged around an older pile from a previous cave-in. "Yeah, yeah I'm here."

"What the freak!" Stacy rushed to him and pounded her balled fists on his chest.

"What?" he asked.

"Why didn't you answer?" Matt asked. "We were getting worried."

"I was taking a leak and didn't want to get stage fright."

"Dude," Cody said. "Not cool. Not cool at all!"

"Maybe it isn't what's in that building we need to worry about," Darin said.

"Yeah," Matt agreed. "We might actually be safer up on the surface." He glanced at Catherine. Her face had gone white and she shook her head as she stared up at the fractured ceiling.

CHAPTER 9

Matt examined his forearms, where small rivulets of blood seeped out of nicks and cuts caused by the fragments of broken cement that went flying as the slab crashed onto the pathway. He glanced up and then at Cody. "We should keep moving. Some of those slabs of cement hanging from rebar up there don't look too stable."

"Right," Cody said. "Giddyap."

After walking in silence for about a hundred yards, Catherine pulled on Matt's arm to stop him, and the others came to a halt behind them. "We should clean up Matt's cuts real quick," she said.

She lowered her pack to the ground and dug out an old first-aid kit. The iodine was mostly dried up, so she poured a little water on a gauze pad and wiped the blood and dirt off as well as she could. She examined her work and sighed. "That'll have to do for now, but you should definitely clean them up better when you get a chance. None of them are too deep or gaping or anything, so that's good."

"Thank you." Matt held his arms out as she wrapped them in gauze. "That feels much better."

"We should probably check out Stacy's foot too," Darin suggested.

"Good idea," Catherine agreed. She gathered up the first-aid kit items, then went to sit by her. "Let me take a look."

Stacy removed her shoe. "It doesn't hurt as bad as before."

"That's good to know." Catherine swabbed what little iodine was left onto her foot. "Remind me and I can do this for you a few times a day."

Stacy nodded and let Catherine do her work.

"There you go," Catherine said.

"Thanks," Stacy said. "Remember those suckers you'd get from the doctor?"

"Yeah," Cody said.

"What I would give to have a Tootsie Pop right now," Matt said.

"I always liked the root beer Dum Dums," Stacy said.

They all reminisced on all the suckers that they missed. From the chalky Smarties lollies to Whistle Pops, they all agreed that they missed their old lives, even the doctor's office.

The group trudged on for another hour and a half before coming to another opening in the ceiling. Matt climbed up and held his breath as he peered out. He couldn't hold back a big smile as he descended, using the exposed rebar as a ladder. He dropped the last few feet. "We're almost there! I think we should go the rest of the way up top in case there aren't any more good holes to climb out of."

"Did you see any . . . activity?" Stacy asked, nervously tugging on a strand of frizzy hair.

Matt shook his head. "Nothing, but it's still hard to see details because of how hazy the air is."

"All right," Darin said, "let's get our masks on and get this trek over with."

Matt was surprised no one argued—especially Stacy. The cave-in must have taken the fight out of her. Or she'd just resigned herself to the fact that danger lurked everywhere, so no one place was any safer than another.

They climbed out and kept going. As the building drew nearer, a nervous energy cascaded through Matt's body, and he couldn't help but walk faster. "It looks like half of it was still under construction," he yelled back at the others. "Looks like a hotel, maybe." He jogged the rest of the way to the pitted circular drive in front of the three-story building. He'd been right—it was a hotel. Well, half of one anyway.

"In the middle of, like, nowhere? This remote?" Stacy asked. "It's either going to be creeptastic, or it was built for the ultra-wealthy."

Matt's lungs burned as he sucked in air through the mask, then forced it out again. Maybe jogging hadn't been such a good idea under the current conditions. He stood looking up at the lavishly carved columns holding up the awning across the drop-off area and the entrance to the hotel while his friends caught up to him.

"Is that, like, the ocean?" Stacy asked, staring out past the building.

"The ocean?" Matt turned to look in the direction she faced.

As if of one mind, the group walked toward the black sand of the litter-strewn beach. A slight chill ran down Matt's back as he took in the sight. The water churned and bubbled instead of lapping at the shore in waves like the ocean should. Or like it used to.

Catherine stepped up beside him, their arms brushing. "It's so . . . sad. All the dead fish on the shore and floating in the water. Garbage. Parts of buildings."

Matt nodded as his eyes took in a large section of a roof, a couple of windows still attached, half in the churning water and half on the beach. Chunks of plastic, garbage, plywood, and other detritus floated among the tons of dead fish.

"The water . . ." Justin blinked and shook his head. "It's like a continuous megaplume."

"What's a megaplume?" Darin asked.

"A big one was discovered right before we went into the deep freeze. I was fascinated by it; I watched every news story about it. It was in a place in the Pacific called the Juan de Fuca Ridge. It's like, I don't know, boiling water. They thought it was from a hydrothermal vent forming that released a bunch of hot water at once." He ran a hand over his head, dislodging some of his hair from beneath the straps of his gas mask. "This is crazy."

"Yeah," Catherine agreed. "It's like the tide is just . . . gone. Like the Earth is so off-kilter that it messed up even the tides."

"I used to love the ocean," Stacy said quietly. "But not this one. It looks so dangerous . . . and, like, filthy."

Cody turned in a slow circle, then stopped, facing the churning, white-capped water. "Do y'all reckon we're on an island?"

The dried fruit he'd eaten in the tunnel suddenly felt like lead in Matt's stomach. Yeah, he did reckon there was a good chance they were on an island. A real good chance. But where?

CHAPTER 10

Matt led the disheartened group back to the entrance and climbed through the broken glass of the first of two sets of doors leading into the lobby of the once-lavish hotel. He pushed open the second set of doors, glass still intact, and stepped onto a dust-covered marble floor with a large crack running down the center.

"Umm, like, wow. I was right! Ultra-wealthy." Stacy stared up at a huge crystal chandelier, hanging crookedly a few feet from a large hole in the ceiling. "Looks like we've moved up in the world. Five-star accommodations for the A-Team!" She pumped a fist in the air.

Matt smiled even as he followed an imaginary diagonal line from the hole above to a deep hole in the floor, plunging down at least a couple of stories. No escape from meteorites here.

"Yeah!" Justin high-fived Stacy. "*A-Team* is rad! I'm Mr. T." He ran a few steps and jumped over the back of a velvet-like couch, landing on the cushions in a giant plume of dust. He waved his hands in front of his face, coughing like a three-pack-a-day smoker.

"Y'all, look at this." Cody stood in front of a large painting hanging in a gold-embossed frame next to the fireplace.

The others joined him, Justin still hacking up a lung.

"Pangea . . ." Matt read out loud. "You were right, Cody, we are on an island. An island named Pangea."

"Pangea?" Catherine asked. "I've never heard of an island with that name."

"I'm sure there's a lot of islands out there you've never heard of," Justin said.

"That's true," Catherine said. "But what if it's a fake? Like the soundstage? Like HZRD?"

"Good point," Matt said. "Let's keep our guard up. Not that it ever went down. I mean, we know what kinda crap the government has been pulling, so just watch out for signs. I hope it's not fake."

Cody nodded and pointed to a building labeled "Hotel Isla Pangea" near the beach. "This is where we are."

"At least it isn't *Hotel California*," Catherine said. She looked around at her friends. "You know, like the Eagles song?"

"More like *Island* California," Matt whispered, "where you can never leave."

A small company logo painted in the bottom left corner read "Demo Trench."

"Look at all the hotels." Catherine pointed to several of the extravagant buildings in the painting. "And neighborhoods? Stores? Are these all really here, on this island?"

Darin shook his head. "I think this is more of a design plan, like this is what it would have looked like if they'd been able to finish everything."

"Know what I ain't seein'?" Cody asked. "Anything resembling a cryovault."

"Yeah." Matt scratched his neck. "That HZRD building isn't on here either, though."

"That's all top-secret government stuff. This looks more like they were planning a resort," Darin said.

"Crazy." Justin shook his head, then slapped Darin on the back. "But I'm hungry. Think there's any food in this place?"

Matt looked around at the lavish furnishings of the lobby. "Probably caviar and expensive wine."

"Mmm." Stacy rubbed her stomach. "Caviar."

"Ain't that just fish eggs?" Cody asked, smirking. "That's what we in Texas call fish bait."

Stacy rolled her eyes. "I wouldn't expect someone as uncultured as you to have any taste for the finer things in life." She stuck her nose in the air, but couldn't keep up her charade and started laughing.

Cody joined in her laughter. "I will never understand rich people."

Justin wandered over to the front desk, exploring behind it. He flipped a light switch and said, "Whoa," in surprise when some of the lights in the lobby turned on. "How in the hell is there electricity here?"

"Yeah, I didn't see any powerlines or anything," Catherine said.

"Like, the underground had power," Stacy pointed out.

"And the vaults," Darin said.

"True," Matt agreed. "But remember the instruction manual in the control room? That whole area, as well as the vaults, is powered with geothermal energy from volcanoes. Do you think it could be the same here?"

"That's the only logical explanation," Catherine said. "Right?"

Darin frowned. "I do remember Westbrook saying something about natural volcanoes and geothermal something or other. I wasn't really listening to the psycho at that point."

Matt cringed. He mostly trusted Darin's story about Dr. Westbrook not being the hero he'd portrayed himself as in the videos he'd left them, but once in a while, the initial doubt he'd had about Darin crept back in. "Well, whether or not that's the source of power, I'm just glad to have it. I say we spend the night here. Who wants to explore a little?"

"I'm all in with that," Justin said.

The others nodded. Matt pushed off the front desk counter he'd been leaning against. "Okay. Let's just keep the exploring to this general area for now, stay within shouting distance of each other." If there was one thing this place had taught him, it was that even if something seemed completely safe in the moment, it could turn deadly in a heartbeat.

"For sure, chief." Justin saluted him.

Matt followed Catherine toward a couple of doors next to a small dining area just off the lobby. She looked at him before trying the knob, and smiled when it turned. Inside was a small pantry area, the shelves filled with large cans of food. Restaurant-sized cans. And not just the usual fare they'd been eating for days, like canned fruit.

Catherine's eyes lit up as she grabbed a large, unopened can of dehydrated mashed potatoes, and she let out an adorable squeak when she saw the dehydrated eggs next to it. Even the canned vegetables looked good: green beans, corn, peas, carrots. "We can have a three-course meal tonight with these!"

Matt laughed at her enthusiasm and reached past her to grab a can of cherry pie filling. "Four courses. Don't forget about dessert."

"Now we just need water, pans, and a heat source."

"Hey, guys!" Cody yelled. "Look what I found!"

They put the food back on the shelves and hurried down a short hallway, where Cody stood in front of a set of double doors. When they all got to him, he grinned and flung open the doors with a flourish, gesturing inside with a "ta-da!"

CHAPTER 11

The sounds that escaped the throats of the assembled group ranged from squeals of delight to whoops of joy. Matt reached out to touch one of the large mattresses—still in the plastic cover it had arrived in. He did a quick count: fifteen. Perfect.

"Let's pull these out and line them up in the open corner by the map," he said. "I'm going to sleep like a king tonight!"

"Slumber party!" Stacy yelled.

"Oh yeah!" Catherine high-fived her.

They doubled up and carried the mattresses to the corner, arranging them near each other before ripping the plastic off. Cody turned so his back faced one of the mattresses, his heels next to its side. "I'm takin' the Nestea plunge!" He fell straight back, bouncing up a few inches as his body hit the springy surface.

The others laughed. "I love those commercials!" Catherine said.

"Now I'm thirsty," Stacy whined.

"Well, you're in luck," Matt said. "Catherine and I found a pantry full of treasure, including multiple six-packs of soda."

"Well, why didn't you say so?" Justin asked, already heading in the direction of the pantry.

Each of them grabbed a can out of the armload Justin brought back with him.

Darin and Stacy wandered off, soon disappearing from sight, and Justin and Cody resumed their exploration of the spacious lobby and connected hallways.

Matt and Catherine sat on a mattress, talking and sipping the flat, room-temperature soda. Matt retrieved his Trapper Keeper out of his backpack, pulled out a notebook and mechanical pencil, and started to draw the island, looking up at the painting of the map for reference every couple of minutes.

"You're pretty good at that." Catherine scooted closer to him, so their legs touched.

He shrugged and smiled. He momentarily lost control of his hand as the warmth of her thigh, pressed so close to his, reached his nervous system, shorting everything out for a heartbeat. The pencil lead snapped as he pushed it too hard against the paper. "Thanks." He looked up at her. Catherine's face was only inches from his; her breath smelled like stale cola as she exhaled. He was held hostage by her eyes, mesmerized. He dropped the pencil and notebook to his lap and touched her arm as they both leaned in a fraction of an inch. Matt licked his lips, his heart doing the fifty-yard dash around his chest.

"Come see what we found!" Justin yelled, breaking the spell.

"Damn it," Matt whispered as he and Catherine jerked away from each other. He hadn't meant to say it out loud, and his face flushed as he dared a peek at her.

She smiled, eyes shining, and let out a short laugh.

Matt set his notebook on the mattress and stood, offering his hand to help her up. She took it and got up, and instead of letting go of it, entwined her fingers through his. He gave her hand a slight squeeze and smiled down at her, hoping they'd finish later what they'd almost started before being interrupted.

Justin and Cody waved them over to the area behind the front desk. As they got closer, Matt could see an open door down the short hallway behind them. "What did you find, Cody?" he said. "And it'd better be good."

Cody raised an eyebrow at his friend. "A security room with monitors. Most of the cameras are still working."

"Really?" Matt picked up his pace, and he and Catherine followed Cody inside the small room, Justin at their heels. The nine-inch CCTV monitors flickered as they cycled through the different cameras placed throughout the building. Each time the picture changed to a new location, a label appeared at the bottom of the screen: "Elevator South Side," "East Hallway," etc.

"I wish there was a radio in here," Matt said. "I'd love to try to get in contact with the vault, if we could."

"Yeah, I don't see one," Cody said. "Plus, who knows how to use one."

"I don't," Matt said.

"Me neither," Catherine said.

The four of them watched the monitors for a few

minutes in silence. Matt was acutely aware of Catherine's hand in his, their arms pressed together in the small, dark room, and wished it were just the two of them in there, maybe playing seven minutes in heaven . . .

"What are you guys doing in here?" Stacy's too-loud voice made all four of them jump.

Before any of them could answer, she squealed and pushed her way between Justin and Cody to grab a black-and-silver tape recorder off the desk. "This is just like the one I have at home."

"*Had* at home," Justin corrected.

She rolled her eyes. "Whatever." She pushed the "eject" button, and the top of the cassette recorder popped open to reveal an empty tape slot. "We should totally record ourselves."

"What would we record?" Darin asked. "Besides, I doubt it has batteries, and if it does, they'll have died long ago."

"No duh." Stacy flipped the tape player over, popped open a small compartment, and pulled out an AC adapter. "I think we should record an account of our journey so far and leave it for someone to find in the future."

Matt nodded. "Great idea. Plug it in, let's see if it works." He held a cassette tape still in its plastic that he had retrieved from the shelf to his left.

CHAPTER 12

Stacy pressed the "play" and "record" buttons at the same time, and the tape in the cassette started spinning. She smiled. "Testing. Testing. The apocalypse has arrived." She pressed "stop," and the two previously depressed buttons popped up and the tape stopped. After rewinding it, she hit the "play" button and her voice came back to her, repeating her test message.

"Awesome. How do we want to do this?" Matt asked.

Catherine flipped a light on in the dim room. "First, I think we need to bring some chairs in here, this might take a while. Then I think Cody should start, since he was the first one out of his pod."

"Actually," Stacy said, "Lance-Darin was the first one out of his pod."

Darin smiled but shook his head. "Yeah, I was out, but I was unconscious for two days. Cody should start, and we can all chime in as the story moves along. Just like we're having a conversation, instead of some official-sounding log."

They gathered up some chairs from the dining area and jammed them into the room—a couple of them half-in and half-out of the doorway. It wasn't a perfect setup, but it got everyone as close as they could be to the cassette recorder that sat on the desk. Cody scooted closer to the table, and Stacy counted to three, then pushed the "record" and "play" buttons.

"Hey, y'all. This here's Cody Anderson from the great state of Texas."

Justin snickered.

Cody ignored him and continued. "I don't really reckon I know how many days it's been, maybe a couple of weeks, maybe more, maybe less. I ain't rightly sure. But I woke up when Dr. Westbrook opened the cryopod I'd been in for . . . well, I don't know that either, just that it was a long time. Decades." He looked up at Darin and cocked an eyebrow.

Darin shrugged and shook his head.

"Anyhow," Cody went on, "Westbrook opened my pod and woke me up. He was frantic and said somethin' along the lines of 'we have to get them out.' Before I even had a chance to decipher what he meant, the other pods slipped off the back of the truck and Dr. Westbrook . . . he was smashed underneath them.

"I was disoriented and confused, but I knew I needed help to get those pods off him. The only problem—I didn't know how to open them. Matt's was closest, so I grabbed a tree branch and started pounding on the plexiglass covering the top half of the cryopod. Matt woke up and pounded from the inside, yelling for me to get him out." Cody nodded to him.

Sweat popped out on Matt's forehead as he remembered the ordeal. He leaned closer to the recorder. "Yeah, all I can remember is Cody puking all over the glass, my feeding tube ripping out of my stomach, and feeling like I couldn't breathe. It sucked. Cody finally busted through and pulled me out. Then I puked."

"We couldn't lift the pods with people still in them. They were too heavy," Cody said. "Plus, Catherine woke up and was pounding on hers and crying. So we got her out next."

Catherine smiled at Matt. "And Matt called me Cher, as if I wasn't already confused enough."

Matt's face reddened. "Your hair . . . just . . . reminded me of hers."

She laughed. "We worked together to get Justin out, then the boys slid his pod off the doctor." Her tone turned serious. "He was dead. There was nothing we could do."

"Yep," Cody said. "His whole face was smashed in. He'd lost as much blood as a butchered hog."

"Eww! Gag me with a spoon!" Stacy covered her mouth.

"Sorry," Cody apologized. "While we worked on getting someone else out the hard way, Catherine used her brain and searched Westbrook for a key. Next thing I knew, she'd unlocked the rest of the pods."

Matt scrunched up his face. "She was covered in his blood. I thought for a minute she'd been injured, but"—he looked at her and smiled—"she was just showing her bravery and smarts."

Catherine squeezed his hand. "When we opened the last one . . ."

Matt finished for her. "It was a girl—number seven was on her uniform. She hadn't made it through the crash. Oh yeah, the army truck we were in had crashed."

The group was silent for a few seconds.

Matt started again. "So everyone was out of their pods except Kim—"

Justin let out a single, harsh laugh and pointed at him. "She took one look at your blood-soaked tank top and refused to let you help her with her feeding tube."

"Yeah." Stacy's voice turned sad. "She only wanted Rhett to do it."

"Remember how he walked over to her and just kissed her?" Cody shook his head, a sad smile tickling his lips.

"Those two and their PDA was disgusting," Justin said. "But Rhett was cool."

He and Justin had hit it off right away. Like jocks just instinctively gravitated to each other. Matt nodded. "Yeah, Rhett was cool."

Catherine wiped at a tear trickling down her face. "There were ten of us, eleven counting the dead girl whose name we never knew. This was before we discovered Darin in the cab of the truck." She named all of them, speaking toward the recorder. "So besides me, Matt, Cody, Justin, and Stacy, our group consisted of Kim, Rhett, Victoria, Kyle, and Nathan."

"There are only six of us left," Stacy said softly, "and that *includes* Lance-Darin."

"Five of us are gone." Catherine's voice cracked and more tears plunged from her eyes.

"Let's take a break for a few minutes." Matt reached over and hit "stop."

CHAPTER 13

Catherine leaned her head on Matt's shoulder and he put his arm around her. "Let's go for a short walk," he suggested.

"Okay." She wiped her face and stood.

"We'll be back in five minutes," Matt said. "Then we can start recording again." They walked to the front of the lobby and gazed out at the debris-strewn beach through the glass doors.

Catherine sighed and turned to face him, wrapping her arms around his waist in a tight hug. He returned her embrace and laid his cheek against the top of her head, enjoying the warmth of her body pressed against his.

"I hope this is the end of it," she whispered. "The death. I can't bear to lose another friend."

Matt didn't respond with words, just pulled her closer. He was afraid his voice would betray his jumbled emotions. He'd been hit hard by the deaths in their group. He blamed himself for most, if not all, of them. As the reluctant leader, it was his job to keep them all safe. And mixed in with the guilt and pain was hope—hope that he was closer than ever to finding his parents, and hope in the growing feelings he had for Catherine. His heart raced at the thought, and he gripped her tighter to him.

"Five minutes are up!" Justin yelled.

Sighing, Matt gave Catherine one last gentle squeeze and released his embrace. They walked back to the security room hand in hand.

Catherine put her mouth next to his ear and whispered, "Thank you."

Her warm breath against his neck gave him a chill—the good kind—and he nodded in response.

When they all got situated around the cassette recorder again, Stacy said, "I get to tell this part—the Lance-Darin part." She started the recording. "And now for the best part. We found Lance-Darin passed out in the cab of the big truck."

"Actually, Catherine found him," Justin butted in. "And you said he was gross and wanted to leave him there."

"You said that?" Darin raised an eyebrow at Stacy, half smiling.

"Well"—Stacy stroked his arm and stuck out her lip in a pout—"you were totally filthy. And, like, you had on that lame big belt thingy."

Darin spoke through clenched teeth. "Yeah, the belt with explosives strapped to it, courtesy of the loony, Westbrook."

"That was messed up." Cody shook his head.

"Like, yeah, totally messed up," Stacy said. "But anyway, we named you Lance and put you in one of the empty pods so we could drag you with us to Camp New Beginnings. You and the two dead bodies. Barf."

"We just wanted to give them a proper burial," Matt said.

"You're such a Boy Scout, chief." Justin punched Matt's shoulder.

"It just . . . seemed like the right thing to do."

Catherine gave his arm a squeeze. "It was, Matt."

"And don't forget the damn video tapes," Justin said. "You were obsessed with those. You had to haul them with us to the cabins."

They talked about their first night at Camp New Beginnings. About the generator powered by riding a stationary bike, finding a VCR and TV, watching Dr. Westbrook's videos, swimming in the lake, and exploring the cabins and finding food and clothes.

"Darin was still out cold on day two," Matt said. "I was afraid he wasn't going to wake up and we'd have another body to bury."

Justin snorted. "Yeah, like that worked out so well for the mad scientist and the nameless girl. Shallow graves and a flash flood don't go good together."

Mention of the flash flood darkened Matt's mood. He bowed his head and spoke solemnly. "At that point, I just wanted to go find my parents. I knew there was no one back at the vault taking care of the thousands of people in the cryopods." He swallowed. "So a group of us decided to go back to the truck to see if we could get it running and follow the tracks back to the vault."

"That turned out to be an epic bad idea," Stacy said.

Catherine stiffened. "No one could have known what

would happen. That whole place was like one giant booby trap, but we didn't know that yet. We didn't find that out until much later. What happened was no one's fault."

Matt appreciated her loyalty, but guilt still filled his chest, suffocating him at times. He took a deep breath and blew it out slowly. "Me, Cody, Catherine, and . . . Kyle headed out. The flash flood hit after we'd reached the truck and were trying to fix a flat tire." He ran his hand over his face and buzz-cut hair and whispered, "I had him. I had a hold of him. But the water was too strong, like a raging river—it ripped his hand right out of my grip."

"It slammed that big truck into the trees, remember?" Catherine said quietly. "There was no way you—or anyone else—could have held on to him."

Cody took the reins to finish out this part of the journey. "When we got back to camp, we could see that everything had been flooded. But everyone there had survived."

"Darin finally woke up on day three." Matt glanced up at Darin, then back down at the marble floor. "You had zero helpful information, though. And I thought you were lying about who you were because Dr. Westbrook said in one of the videos that you'd died."

"Freaking crazy bastard," Darin muttered.

"You were frantic to get that belt off." Catherine shook her head. "We had no idea it contained explosives."

"Good thing you kept that key ring you filched off the dead scientist," Justin said.

Everyone nodded.

"And then the snow started," Stacy said.

CHAPTER 14

The tape continued to turn, recording the silence as the group sat, each lost for a moment in their own recollections.

Matt sniffed and rubbed his nose.

Stacy sighed loudly. "Just think, if we would have had winter clothing, we could have built the world's biggest snowman!"

"Or had a mega snowball fight," Justin said. "We wasted all of those snow days moping around, watching stupid videos of some crazy dude."

"Y'all act like this was just a normal, pre-apocalyptic snowstorm." Cody glared at the two of them. "It wasn't. Remember the avalanche?"

Matt dug his fingernails into his hands. Someone else would have to tell this part of the story. He couldn't do it.

"Poor Nathan," Catherine said. "That avalanche happened so fast . . . and he just . . . panicked."

"He was kind of a wimpy dude," Justin remarked.

"Shut up, Justin!" Catherine glared at him. "He was really nice."

Matt stared blankly at the floor, seeing the collapsing walls of the cabin, the huge beam swinging down, bashing into Nathan, the snow burying him. Pulling his dead body out from under it all in the silence of the aftermath. The intense heat that followed, melting all the snow so fast.

"Remember how the trees the avalanche knocked down just popped back up afterward? Like they had springs on them," Matt murmured, still looking at nothing with his glazed-over eyes. "Too bad Nathan couldn't have done the same."

"Ooh, like, he would have been like a zombie. Gag me!" Stacy said.

Matt looked up then, his eyes boring into hers. "Stacy, if you can't take this seriously, maybe you shouldn't be adding to the recording. Joking about the dead is not cool."

She rolled her eyes. "Whatever. Just trying to lighten the mood."

Matt shook his head and resumed staring at the floor. Catherine rubbed his back with slow, steady strokes. Her touch revived him, reminded him that they had survived together and were closer than ever to finding the vault . . . and his parents. "We found the Sev right after that—"

"The R and D," Stacy corrected him.

"Call it what you want," Matt said. "I prefer the Sev."

"Me and you and Catherine found it when we went to look for Kyle's body," Cody added.

Now it was Justin's turn to feel the weight of the

deaths taking its toll on his psyche. He slumped down in his chair. "We deserved that party in the Sev after what happened when you guys got back to camp."

"You want to record that part, Justin?" Catherine asked.

"No. But I will anyway." He jumped to his feet and paced in the small space as he talked. "We took you guys out to see the big junkyard, or giant chem lab thing we found. And while we were dinking around, the sky turned black, and tornados—huge ones—came out of nowhere. Texas Boy told us to find shelter and get low, and we all dove behind one of the big gears stuck in the ground. All of us but Victoria—she huddled up under a tree." Justin wiped his hands over his face. "She saw us and tried to get to us . . . but . . . but a huge piece of glass or something cut her leg. And Rhett, the big idiot—" His voice faltered. "He ran out in the middle of the flying glass and metal and . . . and *trees* for hell's sake! And tried to help her."

Matt's head filled with images from that day. The surrealness of those enormous trucks and gears and glass beakers that seemed like they belonged in the land of giants from a sci-fi book or something. He crushed his eyes shut, but that made it worse. Black tornados swirled on the backs of his eyelids. He held his breath as Justin continued.

"She crawled toward Rhett. But before he could reach her, the wind picked up a truck, and he ducked when it flew at them, but she didn't. It . . . it . . ." Justin closed his eyes and shook his head.

Cody stood and put a hand on Justin's shoulder. "It killed her. That's all we need to say."

If only that was all Matt's internal movie projector would say. But instead, he saw her head, black hair flying all over, as it rolled toward them.

Justin's eyes were vacant as he nodded. "Yeah. It killed her. Then a big piece of metal blew into Rhett as he tried to make his way back to us. He was still alive, but as he crawled—" His voice hitched again. He and Rhett had been tight. "A tornado snatched him up . . . and he was gone."

Stacy sighed. "Kim went all kinds of crazy. When the storm ended, she just wanted to stay there."

"Maybe we should have let her," Catherine whispered. "The way she died was . . . brutal."

"She was my friend, I'll tell this part," Stacy said. "As we got back to camp, a volcano erupted and started shooting, like, hot lava blobs all over. Almost all of us got burned. My foot almost got burned off! Lance-Darin had to carry me." She looked over at him lovingly. "Everyone jumped in the lake except me and him. We stayed on the shore and I put my foot in. The lava started falling like crazy into the lake, so everyone got out . . . except Kim. She was being a stubborn baby."

Stacy wiped her cheeks with her arm. "A big chunk hit her right in the face. Her face, like, *melted*. Like, she looked like Sloth from *Goonies*." What started as a laugh turned to a sob, and she blubbered out, "She died!"

"Like I said," Justin added as he sat back down, "we deserved that beer party at the Sev that night."

"When some of us came back to camp the next morning, we found the underground," Matt said. "And I'm tired of talking, so to make a long story short, it was crazy. The whole area—all the disasters, weather, night and day—were controlled in that enormous underground. We almost lost Cody and Darin. We found out it was the HZRD Westbrook had talked about in his tapes. All fake. A training ground for the apocalypse."

Catherine picked up from there. "We found blueprints and made our way to where we thought we could get closer to the vault—and our parents. We took a long and wild elevator ride—sideways—to an air-lock room, then made our way here, to the Hotel Isla Pangea."

Matt sat up straight and leaned forward, focusing his eyes on one of the security monitors. "What's that?"

He pointed to the monitor that said "Kitchen" on the bottom, showing what looked like the prep kitchen. A big lump, indistinguishable in the fuzzy picture, lay right in the middle.

"I don't like the looks of that," Darin said.

"Me either," Matt agreed.

CHAPTER 15

Stacy stopped the recording. "What *is* that?"

They all moved closer to the monitor. Matt squinted, trying to make out the lump. He shook his head. "I can't tell what it is. But I think we should go check it out; I don't think I'll be able to sleep without knowing if it's something that could be dangerous."

"I agree," Darin said.

"Let's go explorin', then," Cody said.

With the memories of death so fresh in his mind, Matt frowned. "We need to stay together, though."

No one argued, not even Justin.

"I thought we'd done a pretty thorough search of the first level, but I guess we missed something," Cody said.

"Yeah, a *big* something." Stacy bounced on the balls of her feet, leading the way down a wide hallway.

Catherine came to an abrupt halt. "Stop. It can't be back there. These are guest rooms. No way they'd have a loud kitchen next to the rooms."

Stacy continued forward. "Trust me, I *know* luxury hotels."

Matt looked back and forth between Catherine and Stacy, but before he could say anything, Darin made the decision for him.

"Come on, guys, we gotta search the whole first floor again anyway. Does it really matter where we start?"

"True." Matt turned to Catherine. "You okay with this?"

"Sure." She smiled at him. "We better catch up. Stacy took off."

Matt and Catherine jogged to catch up with the group a short distance away. He thought of taking Catherine's hand, but held off.

"Found it!" Stacy shrieked. She'd passed all of the guest rooms and stood at the entrance of a narrow hallway. "Not only am I the Queen of Summer, but I'm also the Heiress of Hotels!"

"Nice goin'," Cody said.

"Another title?" Justin groaned. "Chief, why don't you lead the charge and give the Heiress of Summer a break."

"Hotels," Stacy corrected him.

"You sure?" Matt asked. "You found it."

"No way," Stacy said. "I've done my part, right, Lance-Darin?"

Darin pulled her close and kissed her on the top of her head. "For sure."

Matt brushed past them and led the way down the hallway, entering the kitchen. Off to the right was the doorway to a prep kitchen. A wide piece of athletic tape with "JW's Laboratory" written on it in black marker was stuck to the wall next to it. "JW. Jim Westbrook?" Matt asked.

"Dude, seriously?" Justin smirked. "You are so obsessed with Westbrook and the mountain vault, you see him everywhere."

"Yeah, like, what would he have been doing here?" Stacy's laugh was a pitch higher than normal, which made Matt think she might be just as nervous as him.

"Besides," Catherine said, "it's just a kitchen, right? Not a laboratory." She gestured around her at the stoves, ovens, cupboards, and large refrigerator.

Matt shrugged, annoyed at the teasing, and pushed the swinging doors to the prep area open, stepping inside. "Aah!" He couldn't stop the short, girly scream from forcing its way out of his throat. Someone bumped into him from behind.

"What the hell?" Justin looked over Matt's shoulder.

"What is it?" Catherine asked.

Matt stepped closer and decided it was safe. "Come see for yourself."

As the others filtered in, gasping at the sight, he slowly walked around the large exoskeleton. It appeared to be some kind of insect, but Matt had never seen a bug this big before, not even on *Mutual of Omaha's Wild Kingdom*. The whole insect was almost as tall as him. The organs inside were shriveled and completely desiccated. Matt couldn't tell which organ was which. Someone had clearly been dissecting this specimen. For what reasons, no one would ever know. He shuddered at the thought of this thing living, walking around . . . hunting with its claw-like pincers.

"Eww! Disgusting!" Stacy shrieked. "Is that, like, a brain or something?" She pointed to a large jar with some sort of organ floating in clear liquid.

Matt joined her where she stood in front of a column of shelves with different-sized jars sitting on them. Each jar contained a strange organ or insectile body part suspended in liquid. He shook his head in disbelief. "Westbrook really was a psycho mad scientist."

"No duh!" Darin said. "I've been saying that from day one. You just refused to believe me."

"I believed you all along," Stacy said.

Catherine had a hand over her mouth, her face pale. "What on Earth do you think he was doing with all this?"

"Mad-scientist stuff," Justin said. "Probably building a giant-insect army so he could take over the world." He cackled like an unholy combination of Young Frankenstein and the Wicked Witch of the West.

"Seriously, Justin. That wouldn't surprise me," Darin said.

Cody wandered over to a corner of the kitchen, keeping a wide berth around the exoskeleton. "Do any of y'all know how to work a computer? Maybe this thing will give us some answers." He pointed his thumb at a table that had an Apple II computer, a stack of floppy disks, and a printer sitting on it.

"Oh! *I* know how to work a computer." Stacy hurried over to Cody. "I had one of these in my room at home." She reached behind it and flipped a switch to turn it on, then hit the "on" switch on top of the monitor. She clapped her hands when it powered up.

Matt had thought she'd been lying, or at least exaggerating, when she said her family was rich, thought she'd just been trying to one-up Kim, but maybe she really was rich. She'd definitely used a computer before, and only rich people could afford to have home computers. The cost of those things was outrageous.

Stacy flipped through the floppy disks. "What kind of information are we looking for?"

"I don't really know," Matt admitted. "What are those disks labeled?"

She started reading off the labels. "Lab Notes, Schematics, Record—"

"Let's start with the lab notes," Catherine interrupted.

Stacy dropped the pile in her hand with an annoyed exhalation. She inserted the disk labeled "Lab Notes" into the drive and smiled when it started to make a whirring sound. She opened the first file and scooted over so Catherine could see it.

Matt looked through the other floppy disks while the girls read through Westbrook's notes. The monitor was too small for all of them to crowd around it.

"This is crazy," Catherine said, pointing at the screen.

Matt stopped flipping through the disks. "What?"

"He was seriously trying to create monster insects! He was messing around with DNA. He keeps mentioning research done by someone named 'Sanger.'"

"This is totally warped." Justin looked around the kitchen/laboratory and shook his head.

"Yeah," Matt agreed. He looked down at the disk

he still held in his hand, and a jolt of excitement stabbed through his chest. "Stacy, put this one in." He shoved it at her.

"What is it?" she asked.

"It says 'Topographic Map.'"

"You and your obsession with maps," Catherine teased.

Matt smiled and shrugged as Stacy swapped the disks out.

CHAPTER 16

A folder labeled "Formative Stages of Pangea" caught Matt's eye. "Open that one." He leaned in.

It was just a word processor document. Matt put his hand on the mouse and scrolled quickly.

"What does it say?" Stacy asked.

Matt shook his head. "It looks like Pangea was formed when the bomb went off in the Mariana Trench. Seems to suggest the ocean floor pushed upward, causing this land mass. No one knew about it except for the top brass of all the world. Weird." He stood and shrugged. "Okay, Stacy, go to the map."

"Ay, ay, captain," she said, clicking on the folder that said "Map."

A pixelated portion of the island filled the monitor. Matt grew even more excited when he saw that everything was labeled. He pointed to a place marked "J-75 Vault."

"J? How many vaults can there be on this island?" he asked.

Stacy hit the right arrow key and another section of the map came up. "There are, like, six pages to this map."

"Is there a way we can see the whole thing at once?"

"Not on this tiny screen." Stacy looked over at the printer. "Maybe if we can print it out, you can lay the pages out to form one big map."

"Brilliant idea," Matt said.

Stacy turned the printer on—Matt let out a breath he'd been holding when it actually powered up—and checked to make sure the holes on the sides of the paper already inserted in the printer were lined up with the sprockets on either side. The paper already threaded in the printer was connected to a pile of fan-folded continuous paper sitting on the table behind it.

Matt crossed his fingers, hiding the gesture from the others by putting his hand under his opposite arm. Stacy clicked some keys on the computer like an expert, and the printer whirred to life, noisily pulling the paper in through the back and spitting it out slowly from the top as the printing mechanism glided back and forth.

As the images formed on the paper at a snail's pace, Matt thought about Stacy's computer knowledge. He could have taken a computer science class at school, but chose weightlifting instead. He figured computers would never be something he'd need to worry about—they were only for rich people and maybe the government. The closest he'd come to actually using one was his friend's Atari— and that was just a bunch of games. You didn't need to know how to do more than turn it on, insert the game cartridge, and maneuver the joystick to play. Matt was the master of *Space Invaders*. He smiled at the memory.

The printer stopped, ejecting the last page of the map out far enough to tear it from the blank piece of paper behind it along the tiny perforations. Stacy handed the small stack of papers to Matt. "Here you go, Map Boss."

"Can we get out of this creepy room now?" Catherine asked.

"Yes, of course," Matt said. "Let's go back to the dining area so I can lay these all out on a table."

Back in the dining area, they gathered around a table. They all helped Matt remove the sides of the paper where the holes for the printer were so he could lay the sections of the map side by side. Like a puzzle, it took him a few minutes to get all the pieces lined up in the right spots to form a pixelated picture of the entire island.

Cody pointed to a section. "There's the HZRD site."

"And there are a few more soundstage buildings like it." Darin pointed them out on opposite areas of the island. "DSTR, CTRPHE, THRT, and PTFLL."

Matt didn't care about the soundstages—he never wanted to get near one of them again. He searched the map until he was sure he'd found all of the vaults, amazed to count ten of them, labeled A-67 to J-75. He did the math in his head, assuming there were five thousand people in each vault as there were in B-35. "There could be close to fifty thousand people on this island still in cryosleep!" he exclaimed.

"What?" Justin scoffed. "How do you figure that?"

"Look." He pointed at each vault as he counted to ten. "Ten vaults, five thousand people in cryosleep per vault, equals fifty thousand."

Cody whistled. "That's crazy."

"Maybe not all of the vaults have the same number of pods," Catherine said.

"That's possible," Matt agreed. "But still . . ."

Darin stared at the map. "Yeah. That's a lot of people."

"Who cares?" Stacy put her hands on her hips. "We only care about one of those vaults—the one where *our* families are."

"That's harsh," Cody said, adding softly, "Those people have families too."

"Again, who cares?" Stacy said. "We obviously can't help all of them, so the priority has to be our families."

Catherine exhaled slowly. "I understand what you're saying, Stacy. Our choice has to be our own families, but we can still care about those other people's lives."

"Whatever." The slight quiver in Stacy's voice gave her away as she crossed her arms and turned her back on them.

She cared. The aloofness was all an act. Matt was convinced of it.

"Listen," he said, "those other vaults have someone in charge. They didn't have a Westbrook. I'm sure their vaults are fine and running well."

"That's true," Cody said.

Catherine and Stacy nodded in agreement.

Matt turned back to the map and put a finger on the building labeled "B-35," and a finger from his other hand on the hotel they now stood in. "Look, guys. There's a road that leads right to B-35 from here." He traced it for emphasis and noticed that it went near several small circles, each labeled "Geothermal Access Point."

Justin bounced from foot to foot. "I say we head there as soon as we're rested up."

"I'm good with that," Matt said. "But maybe we should check out the rest of the hotel? See what else we can find."

"No way!" Stacy said. "I've done enough today. I'm ready to relax."

"Come on, Stacy," Darin prodded. "Maybe there are some really nice bathrobes in the rooms. Or maybe even a change of clothes."

With this, Stacy's whole mood brightened.

"So it's settled," Matt confirmed. "The search continues."

The others nodded, smiles breaking through on most of their faces. Matt gathered up the pages of the map—excitement building at the possibility that he could see his parents within the next couple of days—and put them in the "Maps" section of his Trapper Keeper.

CHAPTER 17

They'd already seen almost everything on the first level, so they headed for the elevators. Stacy, suddenly renewed with enthusiasm, lunged in front of everyone to push the button. Only one of the elevators came to life; the other sat silent. The doors whooshed open and the group stepped in—Catherine with hesitation.

Matt put a hand on the small of her back and whispered, "This is just a normal elevator, nothing to worry about." He figured she was thinking about the one-and-a-half-hour horizontal elevator trip from the HZRD underground to the air-lock room. She came very close to hurling her guts out toward the end of that ride.

She turned her head and smiled shakily at him, nodding.

"Let's go floor by floor, start low and work our way up," Cody suggested.

He reached to press the second-floor button, but Stacy beat him to it with a smirk on her face. "Ha! Beat you!"

"Why are you acting like a child?" Catherine asked.

"Hey!" Darin scowled at her.

Stacy's smile faltered a little. "It's just something we used to do, my brothers and sisters and me. We always raced to see who could push the button first." She ran her fingers down the buttons, careful not to push any as the elevator ascended. "I was the baby, and I beat them there more times than I didn't. I think they let me win." She wiped at her eyes.

"I'm sorry, Stacy," Catherine said. "I didn't mean to snap at you. That's cool about you and your siblings."

Stacy sniffed and stood straighter, nose in the air. "Of course, the hotels we stayed at had, like, a zillion more floors than this. And we usually stayed in the penthouse."

The elevator came to a stop and the door opened with a warbling ding. They stepped out into a carpeted foyer with hallways running perpendicular to it on both sides.

Matt touched the textured golden wallpaper, tracing the white velvet floral pattern with a finger. The gold trim around the elevators, windows, and built-in shelves was flaking off in places. He bounced on his toes, enjoying the cushion the plush carpet provided. "It's been a long time since we've actually stood on carpet."

Catherine and Stacy looked at each other and grinned, both dropping to the floor to remove their boots so they could walk on it barefooted.

"Girls are so weird," Justin said.

"How does it feel?" Darin asked.

"Soft and cushy." Catherine skipped across the foyer to one of the hallways.

Stacy sniffed and wrinkled her nose. "This carpet smells like mildew, though." She stood and shrugged.

"But it still feels good to walk on it. Gives my sore foot a break from my shoe."

The girls put their boots back on, and the group explored the second floor. Some of the guest rooms were fully furnished, but most of them were empty. The only other thing on the floor was a small housekeeping closet with a fully stocked, wheeled cart inside.

"Do you think this place actually had guests stay here?" Catherine asked.

"I doubt it. They wouldn't let people stay here until the construction was finished," Darin said.

"Some of the rooms look like they've been used, though."

Matt nodded. "I noticed that. I bet the construction workers and architects stayed in these rooms. I mean, where else would they have stayed?"

"That makes sense," Cody said. "Hey, do ya'll suppose the showers work? And the toilets?"

Both Catherine's and Stacy's eyes widened and they bumped into each other trying to get through the nearest room's door. Matt smiled as the familiar sound of a toilet flushing met his ears. Stacy whooped when she twisted the faucet and water sprayed from the showerhead.

Stacy poked her head out of the bathroom. "Why don't you boys go finish searching the rest of the floors? I'm going to take a shower!"

"No way," Matt said. "We aren't splitting up."

She cocked her hip and fluttered her lashes. "You just want to watch, huh, Matt?"

His face turned as red as the carpet, and he sputtered,

"No . . . I . . . of course not." He could not even look at Catherine.

"I'll watch," Justin offered. "Hell, I'll even help." He raised his eyebrows.

Darin puffed up his chest and stepped toward him.

"Just joking! Don't go all ape on me, dude. I'm a perfect gentleman, for real."

Matt had to get control of this conversation before chaos broke out. He looked to Cody for help.

"How about we finish our search, just to make sure there ain't no monsters lurking about, and then we can stand outside the rooms while y'all shower. Heck, we all need to shower." Cody looked down at his dirt-and-ash-covered clothes and exposed skin. "We can take turns."

Stacy's smile faded, but she agreed. "Okay. But let's get on with it. I'm not going to wait all night."

After a brief argument, they decided to check out the third floor before going back down.

"It seems like we're just going to find more guest rooms up here," Darin grumbled as the elevator doors closed. "Why waste time looking at identical floors?"

Matt actually agreed, but he wanted to explore every inch before going back down. They'd missed the kitchen upon first search. He didn't want to make the same mistake twice. He rounded a corner, and his gut instinct was correct. Matt smiled. In front of them was a partially wallpapered area, and the uncarpeted floor was covered with painter's plastic. He peered down the hallway at bare boards and construction materials strewn about.

He walked toward a pile of lumber, the others following behind him. "Jackpot!" he exclaimed as he walked faster.

"What?" Cody asked.

"Blueprints!" Matt picked up the stack of papers that had been draped across a couple of sawhorses. He spread them out on the pile of lumber, flipping through and skipping over the areas they'd already explored.

"There's a lot more to this place than we thought," he said.

CHAPTER 18

Matt had to admit that a warm shower felt amazing. He laughed again as he thought about the cry of joy that had come from Catherine when actual hot water had sprayed from the showerhead. He and Cody had been standing just outside the bathroom, and laughed as Catherine explained through the door what her excitement was about.

Justin and Darin stood guard in the room next door as Stacy showered—for twice as long as Catherine.

"I wish we had clean clothes to put on," Catherine said as the freshly washed friends took the elevator back to the first floor.

Matt couldn't take his eyes off the glowing pink skin of her face; her happy, sparkling eyes; her long, wet curls bouncing down her back from one side of her head, the other being shaved from the burn. Then there were her perfect lips . . .

She smiled a smirky smile, and Matt knew he'd been caught. He licked his lips as warmth rushed up his neck into his face. He met her playfully glinting eyes, shrugged one shoulder, and smiled back.

Back in the lobby, Cody and Catherine volunteered to go to the kitchen and cook some of the dehydrated food they'd found. Darin and Stacy had disappeared again. Justin stayed with Matt, who spread the map out on his mattress so he could double check the route they'd need to take to the vault. If it were up to him, they'd leave first thing in the morning, but the others had voted to spend one more day at the hotel, getting some much-needed rest and preparing supplies.

A rattling noise came from the hallway leading to the kitchen. Matt and Justin looked up to see Cody and Catherine pushing a two-tiered metal cart loaded with freshly cooked food.

Justin sniffed the air and jumped to his feet with a big grin. "Whatever you guys made smells bitchin'!" He rushed to help them push the cart over to the mattress corner.

Matt stuffed the papers back into his Keeper and stowed it in his backpack. "It really does smell fantastic."

The wafting odor of hot food brought the lovebirds from wherever they'd been hiding. "Do I smell eggs?" Darin asked.

"Why, yes, you do," Cody answered with a smile.

Catherine handed out plates and forks to everyone. "Serve yourselves." She removed the lid from a pot full of mashed potatoes and handed a serving spoon to Justin, who was, of course, first in line. Then she lifted the lid off of a large, deep frying pan full to the brim with scrambled eggs and handed a big spoon to Matt.

"Eww. Like, mashed potatoes and eggs do *not* go together," Stacy said.

"Then don't eat them," Catherine responded.

Stacy stuck her bottom lip out in a pout. "I never said I wasn't going to eat them. I just said they don't go together." She bumped Catherine's hip with hers. "But it smells totally rad. Thank you for cooking."

The tension in Catherine's jaw softened and she smiled at Stacy. "You're welcome. And there's cherry pie without the crust for dessert."

Matt laughed. "The filling is the best part anyway." He and Catherine filled their plates, then sat together on his mattress to eat.

Even without gravy or a big blob of butter, the potatoes were the best Matt had ever eaten. By the time he finished a pie's worth of cherry filling, his stomach was more than full, and his abs hurt from laughing with Catherine as they talked about their high school experiences before being frozen.

Catherine's hair was now dry and lay in shiny black curls over one shoulder as she lounged on one elbow on the mattress. She pushed a strand out of her face, sat up, and removed the elastic hairband from around her wrist. As she reached up to pull her hair back, Matt stopped her with a hand on her arm.

"No. Leave it down, please. I like it." He moved his hand from her arm up to tuck her hair behind her ear, brushing his fingers across her cheek in the process. "And . . . I like you. A lot."

She put the hairband back on her wrist and smiled, scooting closer to him. "I like you too. A lot."

Matt's stomach flipped and he looked around quickly. Cody and Justin had taken the cart back to the kitchen, and Stacy and Darin lay on a mattress away from Matt's, lost in their own world. Looking back into Catherine's dark eyes, he readjusted to face her more fully. He swallowed and almost went into cardiac arrest when she licked her lips, then parted them slightly. He wove his fingers through her hair and rested the palms of his hands on the sides of her face, pulling her gently to him. He tilted his head and closed his eyes as their lips touched. Then he was lost. Everything forgotten except the sensation of her lips responding to his, her soft hair tangled in his fingers, and her hand resting against his chest.

CHAPTER 19

With the mattresses all pushed together into one giant "mega-bed," as Stacy called it, they settled in for the night, everyone on their own mattress. The only light came from a small lamp on the front desk across the room.

"Are you guys sure we need to stay here another day?" Matt asked as he stared up at the ceiling. "I think we should head out to the mountain tomorrow, to the vault."

Stacy sighed. "After knowing how wonderful these mattresses feel against my battered body, like, I'm especially certain we need to stay another day—at least."

Matt propped himself up on his elbows. "One day—maximum." No way was he going to stay here any longer than that, not with his parents so close.

"Chill, Matt, I was just joking. Mostly," Stacy said.

The mattresses were amazing, he had to admit. Matt rolled to his side and smiled at Catherine, who lay facing him on her own mattress. She smiled back and winked. He wasn't sure how to respond to that, so he just laughed and winked back. He didn't have much experience with girls. The girls in his high school tended to go for the jocks, and he was more of a nerd with jock potential—except he really didn't like to play sports. He did know that the kiss he and Catherine had shared was mind-blowing, at least for him. And he couldn't wait to be alone with her and do it again. He flopped onto his back and sighed. His thoughts were interrupted by Cody.

"Why do y'all suppose there's so many hotels on this island?"

"Good question," Darin said. "Do you think any of the others are finished? Maybe the people who were in training for the apocalypse stayed there."

"Yeah, maybe," Cody conceded. "I was also wonderin' why we never heard about this island. You'd a thought at least a fisherman or two would have seen it, that the news would have investigated it."

Justin yawned. "I bet the Navy controlled the water all around it, so nobody could get close enough to see what was going on."

Catherine nodded. "That sounds legit. Wouldn't the Navy have had to bring all the supplies to build everything, anyway? I mean, how else would the government have gotten everything here?"

"Like, those aircraft carriers are mega huge," Stacy said. "They could've brought all the giant equipment we've seen."

"I think you're right." Darin smiled at her. "I don't see how else it could have been done. This place took a lot of mobilization and manpower to create."

Justin yawned again, and they all quieted down. Matt fell asleep with thoughts of Catherine floating around in his head.

CHAPTER 20

The first thing Matt did the next morning was get the folded-up blueprints out of his Trapper Keeper. "I thought I saw something interesting on here before I got distracted by the kitchen." He flipped through the pages and pulled one out. "Here."

"What is it?" Catherine put her hands on his shoulders and leaned over him as he kneeled in front of his mattress.

He touched one of her hands with his and smiled up at her. "It's an outbuilding. A big one. It's labeled 'Emergency Supply Storage,' and it looks like we can get to it without being outside longer than a few seconds. It's only steps away from the back employee entrance. Wanna go check it out with me?"

"Of course." She smiled.

After putting the blueprints away, Matt stood and, taking Catherine's hand, walked toward the back of the hotel.

"Where y'all headed?" Cody caught up and walked beside him.

"To check something out that I saw on the blue-prints."

Matt's disappointment at the interruption must have shown on his face. With a wink and a grin, Cody did what any good friend would do in such an instance. "Well, you two have fun. I'll get the rest of us organized to go search for supplies . . . away from where you guys are 'checking something out.'"

"Thanks, Cody."

"Yep." He loped off to intercept the others.

Matt squeezed Catherine's hand and smiled to himself, his worry about Vault B-35 taking a back seat to the chance to be alone with her for a short time. Guilt at these thoughts caused a pressure in his chest, but he pushed it aside by telling himself that they were going to the storage building to find stuff for the trip to the vault—being alone with Catherine was just an added bonus.

They found the employee entrance down a back hallway near the kitchen and held their breath as they pushed the door open, hoping the adjacent building would be unlocked. It was only about ten yards away, with a regular-sized door facing them. They hurried to it, still holding their breath in the ash-filled morning air, and Matt grasped the rusted doorknob and twisted it. Unlocked!

Air rushed out of his lungs and he hurried to refill them after he shut the door.

Catherine flipped a light switch on the wall. "This place is huge!"

Matt could only nod as his eyes took in the numerous

shelving units, all stacked to the top with supplies. He wandered down the aisle between two rows of shelves, Catherine at his heels, and choked on his own saliva when he got to the end and saw a most beautiful sight—a vehicle that appeared to be in prime condition.

After he coughed so much his face turned red, Catherine patting his back, he grabbed her hand again and headed straight for the Jeep Wagoneer. They slowly circled the forest-green Jeep, Matt stopping to admire the big black grille guard with attached winch. The round KC lights affixed to a bar on top reminded him of his cousin's pickup truck they used to take out mudding on the rare occasions it rained in their small Nevada town. Looking at the tires, he thought that maybe the Jeep was lifted even higher than that truck—which had been nearly illegal.

"Do you think it runs?" Catherine asked, looking into the driver's side window.

"I sure hope so. Can you imagine how much faster we could get to the vault if it does? We should go get Cody before we try it; he knows the most about engines and stuff."

"But last time, all the batteries were gone," Catherine said.

"Good point. Let's look under the hood," Matt suggested.

He opened the driver's side door. "That's weird looking."

"Yeah, like something seventies sci-fi."

The instrument panel was not like the Jeeps he was

used to—instead there were strange screens and toggles unlike anything Matt had seen.

"Um, I don't see the hood latch in here." He stood.

Catherine shrugged. "I don't know either."

"Let's let Cody take a crack at it."

"Ye-ah." Catherine looked at him, her eyes glinting. "But we should explore a little, *alone*, first."

The emphasis she put on the word "alone" made his knees go weak. Matt focused intently on the shape of her lips. He knew he was staring, but he couldn't tear his eyes away. His mind fuzzy, he had trouble forming words. "Uhh . . . umm . . ." He nodded instead and smiled, finally moving his gaze from her mouth to her eyes.

She laughed and led him away from the big garage doors by the Jeep, over to an area with a leather couch, a couple of chairs, and a throw rug covering a small section of the cement floor. They sat next to each other on the couch, Matt hyperaware of every miniscule nerve fiber firing off at once in the areas of his arm and leg that came into contact with hers. Holy cow, he liked her so much. Maybe even loved her . . .

He twisted to face her and put his arms around her waist, pulling her closer as her arms wrapped around his neck. Their lips collided. As they kissed—his hands pressed into her back, one of her hands stroking the back of his head and neck—he knew. He was in love with Catherine. And that scared him worse than anything he'd encountered up to this point in his life.

CHAPTER 21

The air outside the storage building had gone from wind-blown ash to eerily still when Matt and Catherine hurried back to the employee entrance of the hotel. Matt glanced up at the sky behind them, and his body turned cold at the sight of the blood-colored sun. He wished they could have stayed on that couch, tucked safely away from the world outside, for the rest of their lives.

The smirk on Justin's face as they joined the group in the lobby told Matt that his and Catherine's secret wasn't much of a secret.

"How was the make-out session, lovebirds?" Justin asked.

While Matt's face turned red, Catherine shot right back with, "Jealous much, Justin?"

His teasing grin turned to a scowl. "As if," he grumbled.

Catherine nodded. "That's what I thought."

Cody, master of subject changes, asked, "Did you guys find anything?"

Matt perked up, remembering the good news he had to tell them. "Yes! There's a storage building behind the hotel. It's huge. And . . ." He paused for effect. "There's a battle-ready Jeep Wagoneer in there!"

"And a ton of other stuff. Shelves full of food and supplies," Catherine added.

"What kind of supplies?" Stacy asked.

Catherine shrugged. They hadn't really explored much after finding the Jeep . . . and the couch. "Doomsday prepper stuff."

"Let's go check it out," Darin said. "All we found were a few painter's tarps and construction tools, besides the food pantry we already knew about."

Matt and Catherine led the way to the supply building.

* * *

"This is so wicked!" Justin walked slowly down the nearest aisle, calling out the items on the shelves. "There must be thousands of MREs on this row alone, boxes and boxes of them stacked to the ceiling. And canned food, good stuff—they even have SPAM!" He grabbed a box from the shelf and ripped it open, grabbing one of the ten or so tins of the processed meat.

"Eww." Stacy wrinkled her nose. "Like, barf me out. Who eats that stuff?"

"Poor people," Justin said. "I don't expect a snob like you to understand, but this stuff was like the filet mignon of the trailer court."

"Do you think it's still good?" Catherine asked. "It's probably been in here a while."

"Only one way to find out." Justin pulled the key off the bottom of the rectangular can and slid it over the little tab near the top before twisting it all the way around the can to roll up the top section of metal.

"Is it supposed to smell like that?" Stacy plugged her nose.

"Smells like home," Justin said. He turned it upside down and plopped the whole chunk of processed meat and accompanying blob of gel onto his hand.

"Did you make sure the can wasn't dented or swollen before you opened it?" Cody asked.

"Duh, yeah." Justin bit into the SPAM, tearing a huge piece off. He closed his eyes and chewed.

"Well?" Darin asked.

Justin swallowed. "A little stale, but not bad."

"Why don't we all grab something to eat while we're right here?" Matt said. "Then we can eat while we take inventory and mess with the Jeep." He pulled a random box of MREs off the nearest shelf and opened it. He read off the contents of the freeze-dried, airtight packages as he rummaged through them. "Beef stew."

"Dibs!" Justin grabbed it from his hand, having just finished off the whole can of SPAM.

Matt shook his head. "Frankfurters. Diced turkey."

"That one's mine." Stacy held her hand out.

Matt handed the diced-turkey package to her and continued pulling the packets out of the box. "Beef patty. Beef slices in barbecue. Diced beef with gravy." He looked up at Cody, Catherine and Darin with a raised eyebrow.

"I'll take the diced beef with gravy" Cody said. "Sounds like something my mom would have made."

"I'm waiting to see what all the choices are before I decide," Catherine said.

"Me too," Darin agreed.

"Pork patty, ham and chicken loaf—that sounds like SPAM, want it, Justin?" he teased.

"No thanks." Justin rubbed his stomach. "The last one isn't sitting so well." Which hadn't stopped him from ripping open the beef stew package and warming up the main dish with the heating unit that came with it.

Laughing, Matt continued. "Chicken à la king. Ground beef with spiced sauce. That's it for this box. I'll take the ground beef." He looked from Catherine to Darin. "What do you two want?"

"I'll take the barbecue one, I guess," Catherine said.

"Frankfurter for me." Darin held out his hand to accept the MRE.

Catherine watched her friends struggle to open and prepare the food while standing in the aisle between shelves and suggested they all go sit down. She led them past the Jeep to the couch area.

Spirits high, they ate and talked—mostly about the Jeep.

"Do you think it runs?" Darin asked.

Matt looked to Cody, who answered, "Soon as I'm done with this here gourmet meal, I'm gonna find out."

Justin finished before everyone else and walked back to the shelves, a different aisle this time, calling out what he found. "Duffel bags—big ones, like the military uses. A whole slew of canvas tents. Flashlights." He turned down another row. "Hey, there's some walkie-talkies back here."

"Bring some of those for sure," Matt said.

"Toilet paper! Tons of it! And blue tarps!" Justin yelled.

Cody looked at Matt and grinned. "He sounds pretty excited about the TP."

"Well," Stacy said, "I, for one, do not ever want to run out of it."

Licking barbecue sauce off her fingers, Catherine nodded. "Same here."

Justin jogged up to the group, two boxes in his hands. One small and one medium sized. He opened the small cardboard box first. "Swiss Army knives for everyone!" He tossed one to each of them. "And there's a whole section with guns and ammo."

"What's in the other box?" Catherine asked between bites.

Justin opened the flaps. "Oh, these are the radios."

Matt stood. "No, these are *ham* radios." He took a brand-new one still in its packaging. "Yaesu FT-350R." He traced the name and model number on the box. "Does anyone know how to work one of these?"

Matt looked at everyone in the group one at a time, but they all shook their heads no.

There was no way to contact B-35 or the other vaults. Cody put his head down like he had let someone down. "Sorry, Matt."

Matt sat back down to his food and set the radio next to his Swiss Army knife. "It's not a problem. I'll take one with me. Let's just stay the course for now. We know where we need to go."

Cody stood, wiping his hands on his pants. "Let's go check out this Wagoneer."

"We couldn't find the hood release," Matt said, following him. "I checked near the doorjamb under the steering wheel."

"See, that's where they were put years later," Cody said, "but this latch is just above the grille." He went to the front of the vehicle and pulled a hidden lever just between the hood and the grille. A low, thudding click echoed through the storage room and he lifted the hood.

His eyes went wide, and he whistled. "What the heck? This ain't no normal engine."

Matt moved next to him and gazed down, his eyes drawn to a glowing cylinder where the carburetor should have been. "Is that . . ." He looked at Cody. "Is that *nuclear*?"

CHAPTER 22

Stacy stepped back, away from the Jeep. "Nuclear? Like, isn't that radioactive?"

"Well, yeah." Matt looked at Cody nervously, then back at the futuristic engine. "But I'm sure it's shielded—the radioactive part anyway."

"Don't look at me," Cody said. "If it ain't got a gas tank and a carburetor, I don't know anything about it."

"Those batteries are huge." Matt continued to stare under the raised hood. "And why so many of them?"

Cody shrugged.

Matt looked around at the others. All but Catherine returned his look with blank stares or a shake of the head.

Catherine sighed. "The batteries are probably to store the excess energy the nuclear fission makes. You can't turn it off, so it has to go somewhere."

They all gaped at her.

She crossed her arms. "What? I did a science project about nuclear power when I was in junior high."

"So, Matt, your girlfriend's a genius," Justin teased.

Matt's eyes swiveled to Catherine's, and he couldn't help but smile when she didn't correct Justin's use of the title "girlfriend."

"Should we see if it runs?" Cody shut the hood.

"Sure," Matt said.

"You do the honors, Matt, since y'all are the ones who found it."

Matt climbed into the driver's seat and wiped his sweaty palms on his pants. He looked on both sides of the steering column for keys, but there wasn't even a place for a key to go. The dashboard looked more like it came from a spaceship than the local Jeep dealership. He studied the toggle switches and chose the one labeled "Engage Motor" on top and "Disengage" on the bottom, where the toggle was now positioned. He flipped it up, disappointed when the Wagoneer didn't roar to life.

A rap on the window next to him made him jump. *Just Catherine.* He rolled down the window, a little embarrassed by his reaction.

"If you're waiting to hear the engine rumble, that isn't going to happen. Just put it in gear and try pushing on the gas pedal—gently," she said.

"Yeah . . . that makes sense." He pulled the gearshift on the steering column down into Drive, then pushed on the gas pedal, barely. The big vehicle moved forward, toward the garage doors. Matt hit the brakes and put it back in Park as his friends cheered. Finally, something had gone their way!

They spent the rest of the afternoon and into the evening in the supply building. They each packed a duffel bag with supplies.

"How much food should we bring?" Matt asked. "I mean, should we plan on taking enough for whoever might be awake at the vault?"

"We have no idea how many people are awake," Darin said.

Catherine folded and then rolled up a blue tarp as small as she could get it, then stuffed it in her duffel bag. "How about we take some extra, just in case, knowing we can always come back for more."

"What about the other vaults?" Matt asked.

"You are, like, so obsessed, Matthew. Give it a rest." Stacy flopped down on the couch, her duffel only about half full.

"My name is not Matthew."

Cody looked at Stacy with narrowed eyes that said *not one more word, young lady!* To Matt, he said, "We can check them out later, after we see what's going on at B-35. Heck, now that we have transportation, traveling around the island will be a snap."

"What do you think we're going to find at the vault?" Catherine bit her bottom lip, her forehead creased with worry.

"Hopefully our families . . . alive," Matt said.

Darin sat on the carpet near the couch, shoving MREs into every segment of his bag where he could fit one. "I hope so, too, Matt. But . . . I don't know. Me and Westbrook were the only ones there to run things. Alarms were going off day and night." He closed his eyes and slumped against the couch. "With no one there to address the alarms . . ." He shook his head.

Eyes still closed, voice barely above a whisper, Darin

said, "I don't want to go back there. I mean, I know *he* isn't there anymore. I saw his body float by when the camp flooded. But . . ." He put his face in his hands, and his voice became a little wobbly. "The memories are there. How he basically held me captive. Ordered me around. Yelled at me. Threw things."

"Oh, Lance-Darin!" Stacy dropped down next to him on the floor and rubbed his back.

"It must have been so hard for you," Catherine said. "Especially when you were younger."

Darin sat up straight again and ran his hands over his hair. He cleared his throat. "Yeah. It was. All I wanted was my parents. I plotted ways I could sneak into their section and wake them up. But Westbrook never allowed me to go anywhere near them."

The group sat in silence for a few minutes, huddled around Darin. Then Matt shrugged at Cody and followed him toward the back to finish filling their duffel bags. Stacy shot them both an angry glance.

"Guess we ain't being sensitive enough to Darin," Cody muttered. "I've never been good with feelings."

"He has Stacy and the rest of the group," Matt said. "Honestly, I feel like a jerk now for questioning him so much before."

"We can hear you!" Stacy shouted. "Maybe you should apologize to Darin, *Matthew*."

Matt's spine stiffened. He would have preferred to do this in private, but this seemed fitting since he *had* called Darin out in front of everyone. "Look, man, I'm sorry. I really am."

"I . . . it's fine." Darin released a deep breath. "Come on, guys. Let's help Matt and Cody."

The tension in the room slowly dissipated, and they continued filling the bags. After fastening the top of his, Matt picked it up and lugged it to the Wagoneer, even more grateful for the Jeep, so he wouldn't have to try to carry the heavily loaded bag. "Everyone, bring your bags here and we'll get them all squeezed in. Then I think we should go back to the lobby and make one last recording. Sort of a 'last night at the hotel' send-off."

"Last night at Hotel Spectacula," Stacy said.

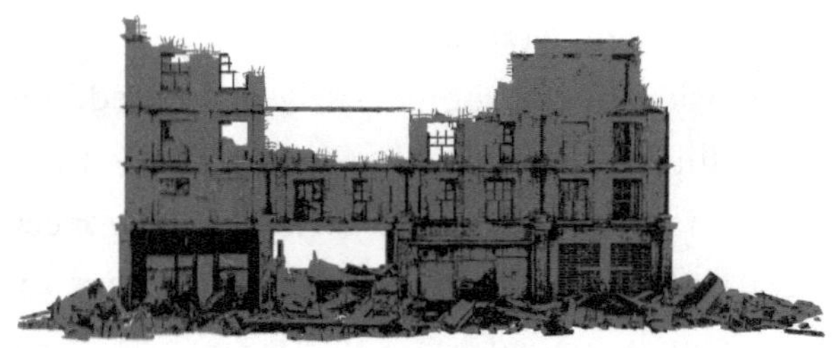

CHAPTER 23

"Matt Voorhees here. This will be our last recording here at the Hotel Isla Pangea—at least for the time being."

Stacy busted up laughing. "You're so Captain Kirk sounding! Do you think this is your captain's log?"

Matt glared at her. He'd had enough of her offhand remarks and rudeness. "Stacy, I'd like for you to leave this room and let me record this last little bit without your comments, please."

"Fine. Lance-Darin and I have better things to do anyway." She grabbed Darin's hand and flounced out of the security office.

After Matt finished, he decided it might be a good idea to have each of them record one last short thought. Catherine went to find Darin and Stacy while Justin started.

"Justin here. Not sure what to say except it was bad enough when Darin and Stacy started sneaking off together, but me 'n Cody are the lone bros now that the chief and Catherine are a thing. All I can say is there'd better be some cute chicks at the vault."

Matt rolled his eyes but didn't say anything. He pointed to Cody.

"This is Cody," the Texan said into the recorder. "It's sure been nice to sleep on a fancy mattress here—I felt like a hog with a brand-spankin' new mud puddle to wallow in!"

Justin and Matt laughed, and Matt paused the recording as Stacy, Darin, and Catherine returned. "You go next, Stacy," he said. He reached for the recorder, but Stacy beat him to it and unpaused it.

"Like, Stacy, giving my last will and testament." She snickered at her own wittiness. "Totally joking! Anyway, this hotel is totally rad—maybe Lance-Darin and I can come back for our honeymoon." She ended by making kissy noises right into the microphone.

Darin blushed and cleared his throat. "Uhh . . . hon . . . honeymoon? But seriously, best two days of this whole messed-up adventure. I wish we were just staying here."

Matt signaled to Catherine that it was her turn.

Staring right at Matt as she bounced a little in her chair, she said, "I'm hopeful to see what the future holds for us. It's gotta be better than . . . I just know we're going to make it." She looked around the room and added, "The six musketeers!"

The others gave a short, spontaneous cheer before Matt took his turn. "This has been a nice break from the horrors we've faced. I will definitely never forget our time here." He looked at Catherine, a small, nervous smile touching his lips. "Tomorrow—on to the vault and our families!"

Matt stopped the recorder. "That's a wrap. We should get some sleep now so we can leave first thing in the morning." With everything ready to go, the Jeep as transportation, and a full belly, he could finally relax. He waited for everyone to get settled on their mattresses and turned off all the lights except the small desk lamp they'd left on the night before.

As he crawled onto his mattress, he smiled over at where Catherine sat on hers. He reclined and put his hands under his head, with his elbows bent out to the sides. Though he was tired and content, the excitement of their journey ahead and the anticipation of finally being reunited with his parents wouldn't allow his mind to rest.

Apparently, Matt wasn't alone in this.

Darin sat up on his mattress and blurted, "I have something I need to tell you guys."

Matt propped himself up on his elbows. "Okay, go for it."

Looking down at his lap, Darin drew in a deep breath. "I . . . I want to tell you what really happened at the cryovault. I haven't been . . . well, completely honest about some things. Matt, you didn't need to apologize earlier."

Stacy gasped.

Matt sat up and scooted so his back rested against the wall. He'd had suspicions all along that Darin wasn't telling the whole truth, and his stomach churned to think what he might have lied about. "Like?"

Everyone waited in silence, the movement of breath going in and out of the room's occupants the only sound for several moments.

Darin swallowed. "The damage . . . from the meteor

strike . . . it wasn't really caused by a meteor. Westbrook made me go outside the vault." He shook his head and ran his fingers through his hair. "He made me climb up on the rocks on top of the vault and plant some dynamite, then I set it off when I got back down to the ground."

"What?!" Matt yelled, standing and stomping off the end of his mattress. "*You* are the one who caused the damage that made our column fail?"

Justin stood, too, his eyes shooting daggers at Darin. "The one that *killed* all of the fifteen-year-olds, including Rhett's sister?"

Darin held his hands out, palms forward, and shrunk into himself. "It wasn't my fault! Westbrook made me do it!"

"Why?" Catherine asked. "Why would Westbrook make you do that?"

Bitterness seeped into Darin's voice. "So he could fix it, of course, and be the freaking *hero*. I didn't . . . I didn't know anything about explosives. I was just a kid! I just did what he told me to do. The blast was bigger than Westbrook thought it would be. It caused more damage, and we were able to eventually fix it with his carbon-foam invention. But it caused other issues—ones we couldn't see. And sometime later, after I was put back into cryosleep, the fifteen-year-olds' column failed. The column wasn't supposed to fail. They weren't supposed to die."

"Oh, Lance-Darin." Stacy's voice was quiet, almost a whisper. "You were just a kid. You said you didn't know! Why didn't you tell me?"

Matt clenched his hands into fists. His heart pummeled his chest from the inside.

Darin wiped at the tears now free-falling from his eyes. "He threatened my family, said he'd pull their plugs and make me watch them die."

Catherine put a hand to her chest. "That's awful. What kind of person . . ." Her voice trailed off as she shook her head.

"A freakin' crazy one!" Darin's voice shook and the tears fell harder. "I'm sorry. I'm sorry I lied and sorry I did what he told me to do. But damn it! Like Stacy said, I was just a kid—a child—scared and alone and afraid for my family."

Unclenching his hands, Matt drew in a few deep breaths. Darin was right. He'd been just a kid. Matt probably would have done the same. And it was tearing Darin up inside—he could see that now.

"Darin," he said, "Westbrook used you. You were just a pawn in his demented plan, just like everyone else. I can see that clearly now. It wasn't your fault. Any kid would have done the same."

Darin looked up at him, his face splotchy from crying. "Thank you, Matt. I'm sorry. I really am."

CHAPTER 24

Sometime during the night, Catherine had rolled to the very edge of her mattress, closer to Matt. Close enough that when he awoke, he found her warm hand entwined with his, and they lay facing each other, only a couple of feet apart. As much as he yearned to get started on their trek to the cryovault, he wanted to savor this moment a little longer. He watched Catherine sleep, her dark curls spread out around her face, her breathing slow and steady.

"Let's get this party started!" Justin yelled as he arched his back in a big stretch.

The magical moment shattered. Catherine pulled her hand away with a start at the loud exclamation. She sat up and ran her fingers through her hair, trying to tame the bedhead, and smiled at Matt. "How long do you think it'll take to get to the vault?" she asked as she wrapped her hair elastic around the ponytail she'd just fashioned.

"If I'm reading the map's scale right, we should be there before nightfall." Anticipation welled up in his chest, and he reached over and grasped her hand. "We're so close. I can't wait."

She squeezed his hand.

Matt's heart skipped. He stood, then helped her up and pulled her close in an embrace full of so many emotions, he thought he might burst. "Catherine, I—" He stopped himself from blurting out his feelings for her. He'd tell her later, when they were alone. Maybe after they reached the vault. "I think we should get going," he finished lamely, still holding her tight against him.

"Okay," Catherine whispered next to his ear. She tightened her hold on him for a too-brief second before letting go and stepping back. "To the Jeep!" She flung her arm, fingers all pressed together, in the direction of the supply building.

"What about breakfast?" Justin whined. "I'm starving."

"We can eat on the road," Matt said. "It's probably going to be an all-day trip. Like twelve to fourteen hours."

"Make sure you have your gas masks!" Darin yelled so they could all hear him.

Everyone grabbed their backpacks that had made the trip all the way from the control room with them.

When they got to the Jeep, Matt went to the front passenger-side door. "Darin, why don't you drive so I can navigate?"

"Okay." Darin climbed into the driver's seat, an excited grin plastered on his face.

Matt opened the door and gestured for Catherine to sit in the middle of the front bench seat, then he jumped in after her. He pulled his Trapper Keeper out of the backpack he'd shoved on the floor between his feet and opened it to the "Maps" section. "The seals on the Jeep's doors seem pretty good. I don't think we'll need our gas masks in here."

Darin agreed. He flipped the toggle switch to engage the motor, pushed the button on the garage door opener hanging on the visor in front of him, and put the Wagoneer in gear as the garage door slowly opened.

Matt gazed out the windshield. The devastation before him came as sort of a shock after spending two days of relative safety inside the hotel. He'd pushed reality to the back of his mind, and now it flooded into the forefront. Darin followed a road heading in the direction of the mountain, dodging meteors and cracks in the ground. The going was slow, but Darin was doing a good job of navigating around the many hazards.

"Watch out for that meteor!" Catherine shouted.

CHAPTER 25

Catherine pointed to a small ball of flame falling near the road ahead.

Darin pushed the brake pedal until the Wagoneer barely crept along as they waited for the impact to hit in front of them several hundred yards. A flash of light at ground level and a rumble in the ground beneath them verified the meteor had touched down. Through the ashen sky, the red sun could be seen, but its light was dimmed to an eternal dusk.

"We should be coming up to a fork in the road ahead," Matt said. "Take the left one."

Nodding, Darin dodged a large crevice in the center of the road. The tires bounced over chunks of asphalt and clods of dirt.

"Try driving on the shoulder next to the road," Catherine suggested. "It looks a little smoother."

"Yeah, okay." Darin maneuvered the Jeep to the dirt beside the broken asphalt.

Catherine was right. It was a less jarring ride for a

while. It was slow going, with all the debris and cracked earth they had to dodge.

"Maybe we should, like, turn on the radio," Stacy suggested.

"We can try," Matt mumbled, looking up from his maps long enough to turn the knob. "But I doubt it'll play anything."

They listened to the static as Catherine spun the dial, trying to find a functioning station. After only getting static on every channel, she turned it off. "I guess we won't be listening to any Wolfman Jack on this trip."

"Ahh, man! I love that dude!" Justin said.

"Who's Wolfman Jack?" Cody asked.

"You're joking, right?" Justin's voice held a note of incredulity.

"Uhh, not really, no."

Justin leaned forward and stared at him around Stacy. "What did you listen to on the radio? Did you even have a radio? Or electronics of any kind in backwoods Texas?"

Cody laughed. "Country-western music, of course. *American Country Countdown* and *Live From Gilley's*—those were the best!"

Justin threw himself back against the seat and shook his head. "Country music? I just . . . I just can't."

"Oh, it's hard to be humble . . ." Cody sang loudly, his Texas twang coming on strong.

Justin and Stacy plugged their ears and moaned while Darin, Matt, and Catherine laughed.

"More like, 'Mamas, don't let yer babies grow up to be cowboys.'" Justin's fake, exaggerated Southern accent made them all buckle over with laughter.

"What kind of music did you listen to?" Cody asked him.

"Dude, the good stuff. Rock and roll! AC/DC, Def Leppard, Black Sabbath, Aerosmith! So much great music."

"Umm, like, yuck." Stacy wrinkled her nose.

"Yuck?" Justin said. "What music do you like?"

"New wave all the way, and pop, definitely pop."

"Favorite bands?" Catherine asked her.

"Tears for Fears, for sure the best. The Cure. And A Flock of Seagulls—"

Darin snorted. "Is that for real? A real band?"

"Yeah," Justin laughed, "it was named after the lead singer's hair!"

Stacy slapped his leg. "Shut up! 'I Ran' was, like, my fave song!"

Justin dug around in his backpack and pulled out a can of pork and beans. "Who has the can opener?"

Catherine retrieved it from an outside pocket of her pack and handed it back to him. He snatched it from her before she realized what he wanted to open with it. "Really, Justin? Do you think that's a good thing to eat when we're all crammed in this small, poorly ventilated space for who knows how long?"

He smiled as he cranked the can opener around the rim of the can, the odor of bargain beans wafting through the Jeep. "What's wrong with beans?" He tipped the now-opened can to his mouth like he was drinking a soda. The Jeep rolled over a large chunk of asphalt at the same time, and sauce-slathered beans and bits of pork plopped onto his face and chest. "Son of a . . . Darin! You did that on purpose!"

Darin shook his head, but only laughed along with the others.

Licking sauce and beans off his fingers, Justin joined them. He wiped his face with the hem of his T-shirt, then finished off what was left in the can.

The group quieted down while they all found something to eat from their backpacks. Catherine handed some dried fruit to Darin so he could eat while he drove.

After a few minutes, Darin slowed the Jeep to a crawl and squinted at the road ahead. "Is that a tunnel?"

Matt looked up from opening his MRE and smiled. "Yes! I know where that is." He handed his packaged meal to Catherine and sorted through the maps in his folder. He picked up one of the papers and nodded, bouncing in his seat a little. "Go through the tunnel. We are totally on the right track."

"Are you sure you're reading that map right?" Justin asked.

"Of course I'm sure." Matt took his meal back from Catherine. "I got a merit badge in Scouts for orienteering."

"Orien-*what*-ing?" Justin asked.

"It's, like, knowing how to read a map and stuff," Stacy said.

"And a compass," Matt added. "Though, we don't have one of those that works."

"What did y'all have to do to earn that badge?" Cody asked.

"Well, I don't know if it's officially approved by the

Boy Scouts to do it this way, but it was kinda like what your dad did for you to learn how to survive. My dad dropped me off in the middle of nowhere with a canteen full of water, a day-pack, a map, and a compass, and said, 'See you in a few hours at the rendezvous point.' It only took me two hours. You should have seen my dad's face when he pulled up and saw that I'd beat him there!"

"That's crazy!" Catherine said. "What if you'd gotten lost?"

Matt shrugged and shoved his MRE wrappers in his pack. "I wasn't too worried about it. I'd had a lot of practice with my dad and my scout troop. But I suppose if I'd got lost, my mom would have called in the Army, Navy, Air Force, and Marines to find me."

"Moms are like that," Catherine said.

Justin grunted. "Ha. My mom wouldn't have bothered to call anyone. She probably wouldn't have even noticed I'd gone missing."

Catherine frowned. "That really sucks, Justin. I'm sorry."

He shrugged. "No biggie. I survived just fine without their 'care.'" He made air quotes with his fingers.

"We're getting close to the tunnel." Cody pointed ahead. "How long do you think it is?"

"I'm not sure, it's hard to tell from the map," Matt said. "But you should turn the headlights on, seems dark in there."

"Oh!" Stacy leaned forward to stare over Catherine's shoulder. "We should, like, totally hold our breath when we drive through!"

"Why?" Darin asked.

"To prevent bad luck, duh, silly. If you can hold your breath all the way through, it protects you from bad luck."

"In that case," Cody said, "hopefully it isn't too long."

Stacy clapped as the tunnel neared. "When I say go, everyone hold your breath until we come out the other end."

As the front of the Jeep entered the tunnel, Stacy yelled, "Go!" And they all played along, holding their breath.

The tunnel was long. Matt could barely see the dim light coming from the exit. About twenty yards from the end, Justin lifted up his right butt cheek and emitted a loud fart.

"Justin! Seriously?" Darin said, releasing his held breath.

Catherine laughed, inhaling just before they reached the tunnel's exit.

Stacy, Matt, Cody, and Justin breathed in as soon as the muted sunlight hit the windshield, and Stacy smacked Justin's shoulder. "Barf me out, Justin!" She plugged her nose and continued to give him the evil eye.

"Well, Stacy," Darin said, "I guess we're cursed with bad luck."

CHAPTER 26

Coming out of the tunnel was like landing on a foreign planet. The terrain went from dirt and ash, rocks and hardened lava to a lush, thick, humid jungle. Matt fanned his T-shirt in and out as sweat broke out on his chest and armpits. "Justin, you reek—and this sudden blast of humidity makes your odor even worse."

"Have any of you ever seen plants like these before?" Catherine asked, fanning a hand in front of her face.

"No," Cody answered. "But then again, I ain't never been to a jungle."

"Well, I have," Stacy said. "We went to Belize for a family vacation once. But these plants don't look the same as they did there."

Darin dodged a huge chunk of asphalt ripped out of the middle of the road. "Maybe it just looks different because of the large holes burned into the leaves from lava dropping on them."

Maybe that was part of it, but Matt thought the huge green leaves looked waxy, almost like they were made of plastic. He looked up at the trees encroaching on the battered road. Broken branches and scorch marks indicated where lightning strikes had hit. "I'm not sure why the terrain is so different here, but it definitely hasn't escaped the apocalypse." He gazed out the window at a tree tipped at an odd angle, half of its roots dangling into a wide crevasse slicing through the earth.

They drove in and out of large patches of jungle, the beat-up road winding through. Darin had to dodge plants and small trees that had grown up through the broken asphalt.

The Jeep bumped over an uneven surface where the asphalt transitioned to a dirt road. Soon, there were no tracks at all to follow, and Darin stopped the Jeep atop the lush greenery. "Where to now?" he asked Matt.

"I'm not sure." Matt rifled through his maps, finding the one that showed this side of the tunnel. "I think there used to be a road here, a dirt road at least. But it's been overgrown." He shook his head. "I'm going to get out and look around for a minute to see which way we should go." He grabbed his gas mask out of the top of his backpack.

"I'm going with you," Catherine said.

"Me too, I need to stretch my legs," Cody said.

They all decided they needed a break from sitting, so after donning their gas masks, they got out of the Jeep. Matt held Catherine's hand and smiled at her, wishing they didn't have to wear the stupid masks so they could sneak behind a tree and kiss.

Suddenly, he stopped.

Up ahead was a large, rusted tube extending up about

six feet from where it sprouted from the ground. Drab olive-green paint had flaked off, littering the ground around it. Corroding rivets held the whole cylinder together. It reminded Matt of the pipes Mario always had to jump on or over or into in the *Super Mario Bros.* video game that came out just before his family was chosen for the cryovault.

He and Catherine walked far enough to determine which route was clear enough to take the Jeep through, then met the others back at the vehicle.

They drove slowly, winding between plants with large leaves, still dodging chunks of lava here and there. Through the trees, Matt noticed another of the tubes coming up out of the ground, and then another.

"What are those tubes?" Darin asked.

"I don't know," Matt said. "We saw one when we got out."

"Look." Catherine pointed to one that was closer to the Jeep than the others had been. "They have ladders hanging from the side. Weird."

"I say we go check it out," Justin said, leaning over Stacy to look out Cody's window.

"Get off me, you dumb jock." Stacy pushed Justin back toward his side of the seat.

"I wasn't on you, bimbo," Justin shot back. "I was leaning *over* you. You just wish I was on you."

Darin stomped on the brakes, jolting them all forward.

"Okay," Matt said, "let's go check out these tubes. Then maybe switch seats when we get back." He looked back at Justin and Stacy.

The ladder wasn't long on the outside—the tube only extended about six feet above the ground—but Matt climbed the first few rungs so he could peer inside the open top of the tube. Blue and green wires as thick as his leg followed the ladder down into the cylinder. They each took a turn climbing up to look inside, but none of them really had any ideas what the tubes and wires were for.

Matt wiped sweat off his brow with his arm, anxious to get moving again. Without a road to follow, it was going to take them longer to get to the vault. A barely perceptible buzzing sound caught his attention, and he looked up in the direction of the Jeep. A swarm of winged bugs flew toward them. Matt's eyes widened. They were huge bugs that he shouldn't be able to see individually at this distance. "Umm, guys." He didn't take his eyes off the large swarm. "We should, uh, get back to the Jeep now."

The others followed his gaze.

"What in the french toast . . ." Cody stared.

"Come on," Catherine urged. "Let's go!"

When they got to the Jeep, Matt and Catherine climbed in back with Justin, and Stacy and Cody sat in the front seat with Darin. Stacy curled up to Darin, her left hand wrapped around his bicep and her right hand resting on his thigh. "This is much better," she purred.

Darin smiled and cleared his throat. "Yes. It sure is."

Stacy laid her head on his shoulder and sighed. "Oh, Lance-Darin."

Twisting in his seat so he could look up at the sky, Matt reached for Catherine's hand and squeezed. "Let's get moving!"

Darin pushed on the gas pedal, and they advanced a little faster.

"Whoa, stop, Darin," Cody said.

Darin hit the brakes. The teens watched as a large group of crawling bugs with segmented bodies passed slowly in front of them.

"Dang." Cody leaned forward, hand pressed against the dash. "Those things are bigger than my mama's English setter."

CHAPTER 27

"They're huge! Like prehistoric bugs or something." Matt put his arm around Catherine's back as she leaned over him to watch the slow procession out his window. She pressed her shoulder into his chest and tilted her head back to smile at him. He bent his head toward her, forgetting about the prehistoric bugs for an instant, not even caring that they weren't alone in the Jeep. All he could think about in that moment was kissing her. His heart sped up as his lips neared hers.

"What's going on? Why did they speed up?" The alarm in Cody's voice broke the hypnotic spell Catherine's lips held on Matt, and he jerked his head around to look out the window.

The bugs, which had been moving at the speed of a teenager on his way to do the dishes, now scurried across the terrain in front of and under the Wagoneer.

"Holy shit!" Justin had his forehead pressed against the window on his side of the Jeep.

Gigantic bugs, the size of a German shepherd or

maybe even a Great Dane, rushed forward on long, spindly legs. The first one to reach the straggler of the crawling insects clamped its wide mouth over the smaller bug's midsection, whipped it in the air, and swallowed it whole. Then it turned into a melee as the wide-mouthed giants hunted and dined on their smaller prey.

"I've never seen insects like this before," Matt whispered.

"No duh, dork," Stacy said. "Like, none of us have. I mean aside from the dead one at the hotel. I honestly thought it was fake."

Matt rolled his eyes at her. "What I mean is, they don't look like any of the insects from before. They aren't just normal bugs that have been enlarged for some reason. They're just . . . different from anything I've ever seen."

"You got that right," Cody agreed. "I say we move on out of here while those big 'uns are still distracted."

Darin pulled the Jeep slowly away from the onslaught. The strange beasts ignored them, intent on either escape or dinner, depending on whether they fell under the guise of predator or prey.

The front tires bounced over a segmented bug corpse and its guts that were spread out around it. The back tires spun in the goo before catching traction and moving forward. They drove past as one of the bigger insects dragged itself into the jungle, several of its spindly legs broken and hanging limp.

"Eww." Stacy hid her face in Darin's shoulder as a big bug bit into its prey, spraying dark-colored ichor from the thing's shredded body.

An odor of fermented grass clippings and animal

feces wafted into the Jeep. Catherine gagged. "What is that smell?"

Matt covered his nose. "Bug guts."

Darin pressed harder on the gas pedal, but the Wagoneer struggled to drive forward over the slippery mess.

"Someone needs to get out and lock the hubs into four-wheel drive," Cody said.

Darin stopped and put the Jeep in neutral. "Who's going to do it? I don't have a clue how to, so I can't."

"I'll do the front driver's side," Matt volunteered.

"And I'll do the passenger's side," Cody said.

Everyone remained silent, watching the big-and-bigger bug parade and slaughter. The insects paid no attention to the humans in the Jeep, too intent on their meal.

Matt sighed. "All right, Cody. Let's get this over with."

Quietly, they each pried their door open in slow motion. Like synchronized swimmers, they ducked down to the slimy ground and crawled to the front tires. Matt twisted the lock on the hub that would secure it into four-wheel drive. Cody did the same on his side.

As they climbed back in and shut the doors, a couple of the bigger bugs noticed them and ambled toward the vehicle curiously. One of them, about the size of a cow and at least as tall as the lifted Jeep, bumped lightly into the front fender purposely, as if it were testing to see if they were a threat.

Darin stomped on the gas pedal as more bugs ran to and bumped into the Jeep. The girls screamed.

"They're chasing us!" Cody yelled.

The large bugs that caught up to them crashed into

the vehicle, thrashing it with their chitinous jaws and front pincers. The Wagoneer shuddered with each slamming insect.

"They think we're prey because we're running from them!" Matt yelled.

The Jeep hit a pile of bug guts and spun out of control. It jerked to a stop facing the oncoming herd of bugs.

"Turn around!" Justin yelled.

Darin cranked the wheel and hit the gas with adrenaline-fueled strength. The Jeep fishtailed, spraying dirt and guts from the tires. He slammed his fist on the steering wheel. "Damn it! Go!" The tires spun, digging a bumper-high trench with the left rear tire. "We're stuck! What should I do?"

Several bugs jumped onto the hood and roof of the Jeep. Catherine screamed and ducked down as the roof dented in toward her with the weight of the huge insects. Matt pressed his hand against the roof in a desperate attempt to keep it from caving in on them. More bugs piled on, skittering forth and jumping onto the collapsing vehicle.

The side windows all shattered at once as the Jeep rocked back and forth. Even the boys were screaming now.

CHAPTER 28

Matt's chest hurt, his heart pounding within it, as more of the giant bugs slammed into the Jeep. No light penetrated the mass of insects now glomming on to the Wagoneer. The screech of armor-like carapace against metal penetrated his ears, stabbing into his brain.

A tire popped and air hissed out, eliciting another round of terror-filled screams from the Jeep's occupants.

"Listen! Everyone listen to me!" Matt yelled. Five pairs of terrified eyes looked at him. "We need to make a plan. We can't just sit here and wait to be devoured."

"What should we do?" Catherine asked, tears streaking her dirty face.

Matt turned in his seat, looking for a way out. The rear window was still intact, and he spotted one of the tubes sticking out of the ground nearby. "Look, most of the bugs seem to be attracted to the heat of the engine, so they're up front. We can crawl out the back and run to that tube"—he pointed—"and hide inside until they leave. Then we can come back and see if the Jeep will still run."

Stacy screamed as a spiky leg stabbed through the busted front windshield and into the dash. "Fine! Let's go!" She climbed over the front seat, pushing Catherine to the side on the back seat, then climbed over that one and into the cargo area where all their supplies were.

"Catherine, go!" Matt yelled.

She scrambled over the seat and huddled down next to Stacy, their arms wrapped around each other. Darin and Cody climbed back next as more legs gouged the steering wheel and dash just inches from where they'd been sitting.

"Someone needs to open this window!" Cody searched the back panel for a switch of some kind.

"There's a toggle switch on the instrument board," Darin said. "Someone's going to have to go up there."

Justin took one look at the damaged steering wheel and dash and shook his head. He joined the others in the back, now squished together like cattle going to the slaughterhouse.

"I'll do it," Matt said.

He climbed to the front seat and dodged to the side as a spiked leg stabbed toward him. He hunkered down, trying to avoid the serrated, sword-like appendages using the front seat as a pin cushion. He pulled the toggle switch down and the back window opened less than an inch before stopping. Catherine slapped the palm of her hand against the glass and tried to force it down as the little motor whined uselessly. "It's stuck!" she yelled.

"Hurry up!" Stacy shrieked.

"I'm trying!" Matt toggled the switch up and down to try to get the window moving.

A spike-covered leg hit him in the arm, throwing him back and pinning his shirt sleeve to the seat. Blood trickled down his arm where the barbs grazed it. He struggled, pulling on his sleeve to free himself.

"Matt, what's wrong?!" Catherine cried. "Get back here!"

"I'm stuck! My shirt is pinned to the seat." He grunted with the effort of trying to free himself. Between the stress, intense heat, and high humidity, Matt was slick with sweat.

"I'm coming!" Darin climbed to the front and kicked the monster's leg at a joint. A jet of pale-yellow insect blood sprayed from the amputated limb, covering both him and Matt.

The bug backed away with a high-pitched scream. Matt grabbed the lower part of the leg, still pinning him, and wiggled it out of the seat. He dropped it to the floor, then tried the switch one more time. But the window was stuck.

A jarring crash hit the roof as another giant insect jumped on. The back window shattered from the added weight. The pillars holding up the Jeep's roof finally gave up and started to bend under the pressure. The roof crushed down inch by inch.

"Go!" Darin, already back with the others, pushed Stacy and Catherine out.

"What about the packs?!" Cody yelled over his shoulder as Darin prodded him out the window.

"I'll get them. Justin, go!"

Matt leaned over the back seat into the cargo compartment. "You go, Darin. I'll get these."

Darin nodded and dove out the narrowing space where the window had been. Matt climbed over the seat and pushed the packs out one at a time into Darin's waiting hands.

CHAPTER 29

Darin held a hand over his mouth and nose. "What about the gas masks?"

Shaking his head as he climbed to the back of the Jeep, Matt yelled, "No time!" He rolled out the window, grabbed a pack, and ran toward the pipe, gesturing for the others to follow.

A bug the size of a small dog nipped at Matt's leg, and he sent it flying with a kick. Cody stomped on one next to him. The horde of insects turned to them, homing in on their prey.

"We need to get to the pipe!" Matt yelled.

He and Cody reached it first. Matt kicked and stomped as the horde tried to take bites out of them. He followed Cody up the ladder and over the lip of the tube, both waiting there to help Catherine, and then Stacy, climb over first.

After they descended farther down to a walkway that coiled around another tube to make room for Justin and

Darin, the four of them looked up. It looked like Matt and Cody were the only ones who grabbed a pack.

Stacy screamed, swatting at a smaller bug that followed them down the tube. Another dog-sized bug crawled over the lip of the pipe, its insectile eyes darting from target to target. A huge bug snatched the smaller one and swallowed it whole.

"Hurry!" Matt yelled, glancing briefly down at the girls, then back up as the giant insect clambered over the lip of the pipe, trying to crawl inside.

The girls scrambled down the tube, staring up and screaming as the bugzilla, too big to enter the tube fully, chomped its giant maw in their direction. Drops of spittle the size of golf balls rained down on them.

Matt stared, frozen in a temporary state of shock as slimy extensions shot from its open mouth toward them. A scream caught in his throat as one of the mouth tentacles snagged Darin and jerked him from the tube.

Screaming, Stacy leaped for Darin, grabbing at his leg. "Lance-Darin! No!" She sobbed and screamed while Catherine pulled her down and hovered over her, protecting her from the insect and from her own impulsive actions as she clawed at the tube, trying to get to Darin even after he had disappeared over the rim.

Matt rushed back to the top of the tube.

Darin roared and kicked at the giant insect as it dragged him away.

"No!" Matt screamed, his mind fragmented into a million simultaneous thoughts. He lifted himself just over the lip of the pipe. A shadow darkened the ground below him, and he ducked just as a flying bug swooped down, dagger-like jaws clamping shut mere centimeters from his head. If his buzz cut had been any longer, it would have gotten away with a clump of his hair.

"Matt!" Catherine shrieked among the screams and yells of Justin and Cody.

He ignored their pleas and stuck his head above the rim again, desperation tearing at his insides like a wood-chipper. He caught one last glimpse of Darin's feet, now dragging limply, his blood painting the bug-entrail-covered ground red as the giant predator dragged his friend into the jungle foliage. Smaller bugs scurried all around, many of them following the successful hunter, likely hoping to score the leftovers. Matt's stomach lurched as the thought of his friend being torn to bits, consumed by the abhorrent creatures, forced itself into his mind like a fast-growing tumor.

"Matt! Get down here!" Catherine's frantic voice broke through, and with one last look at the smashed Jeep, covered in bugs, plumes of smoke rising from the crushed engine, he ducked back inside.

When he reached them, Stacy looked up at him, her face a mess of snot and tears, her eyes still carrying a trace of hope.

Hope that Matt crumpled with the shake of his head. "He's gone."

"Are you sure?" Justin asked. "Maybe we should—"

"I'm sure." Matt spat the words. His anger at losing another friend, another life, boiled over. His voice shook. "He's gone." He glared at Justin. "And going back out there—" His voice broke, and he slammed his fist into the wall of the tube. "They're everywhere. Thousands of them. Like they came just to get us."

"C'mon, then." Cody urged Matt onward with a hand on his shoulder. "There's only one way to go for now."

"But . . . no!" Stacy cried. "He can't. This is a nightmare. A nightmare! I just need to wake up!"

"I know," Catherine said, her eyes full of unspilled tears. "I'm so sorry, Stacy. I can't believe this. But we have to move. Remember how Kim almost got us all killed in that forest after Rhett? We can't do that again. Please. We can cry, *all* of us can cry together, when we're safe."

"We'll never be safe." Stacy reluctantly resumed climbing down the tube.

The tube changed from a solid green material to clear, see-through material as they descended below ground level. The large tube shifted over at this point, and began a slow twist around a huge column made of rock. Lights were embedded in the tube above them every ten yards or so. The blue and green wires, each at least six-inches in diameter, continued on inside the tube. Except for the small protrusions every couple of feet along the mild slope, it reminded Matt of a waterslide as it slowly wrapped around and down the rock column. It was easier at this point to sit down and scoot along. Even though the slope was gentle, it was an odd angle to try to stand and walk at.

"What in the . . ." Cody stopped, staring out into a foreign, underwater world.

CHAPTER 30

Like humans in a reverse fish bowl, they were surrounded by water. Strange-looking fish swam by, barely giving the humans a glance inside their tubular air aquarium. Matt gazed out at multiple columns of rock that seemed to go from just beneath the island down to the floor of the ocean. *Like a multi-stalked mushroom cloud*, he thought. Like the columns were what held the island above the water.

Each of the rock pillars had a similar clear tube wrapping around it and cross sections that traveled from one twisting tube to the next, so you could get from one to another without going back up to the island.

Matt swiped his arm across his forehead, now dripping with sweat.

"It looks like a double-helix DNA strand," Stacy whispered.

Matt nodded, not taking his eyes from the alien sight.

"A double what?" Justin asked.

Even in her period of deep mourning, Stacy was able to roll her bloodshot eyes. "Freshman biology, ditz."

Justin stiffened. "Yeah, well, the cheerleaders took turns doing my homework for me so I could concentrate on football."

Cody changed the subject. "It's hotter than a Texas July in here."

Matt turned to examine the column their tube wrapped around. His gaze followed the thick wires down a couple of feet to where they entered the column through an airtight, watertight conduit. The wires returned to the clear tube in the same manner about a foot later. "Do you think these rock columns are full of lava or something? Like that's where the island is getting its power?"

Catherine squinted out at the forest of identical pillars. "Didn't one of the manuals we looked at say something about geothermal power?"

"Yeah. I remember something about that," Justin said.

Cody slapped Matt on the shoulder. "I think you're right, boss. And that explains why it's hotter than Hades in here."

"I think these columns are holding the island up too," Matt said. "I mean, how else would you explain the physics of this thing? Islands don't just float on top of the ocean. They grow out of the ocean floor like mountains."

"Curiouser and curiouser," Stacy whispered.

The boys looked at her like she was speaking a foreign language, but Catherine smiled slightly. "*Alice in Wonderland*. One of my favorites."

"Mine too," Stacy murmured. "And very fitting for

this whole ridiculous situation." She wiped tears from her face with both hands.

"So where's the lava coming from?" Justin asked.

"Deep ocean volcanoes," Matt answered. "They're all over the place. They were even before the apocalypse. And they constantly emit energy."

Catherine scooted up to where Matt sat staring out into the ocean and laid her head on his shoulder. "The ocean has always been like a whole different planet . . . but this . . ." She shook her head against him. "It's like a whole different universe. Maybe it explains what we saw above. Like some sort of pocket of heat and humidity that, I dunno, makes a perfect environment for giant plants and bugs. Matt said it himself—they were like prehistoric bugs. Seems like the right climate anyway."

Matt nodded as a gigantic mutant creature swam around one of the distant pillars. It sort of resembled a whale, but with tumor-like protrusions growing on its body, each emitting spurts of small bubbles at different times. Beneath them, in the deep water, a creature resembling an octopus glowed in the dark. An old, rusty barrel floated by. As Matt watched, the cephalopod wrapped an incandescent limb around the steel barrel and collapsed it like it was made of paper.

The tumultuous white caps they'd seen from the beach near the hotel presented below as fast-moving water funnels—like underwater tornados, with releases of air in large bubbles boiling from the sea floor, and a constant motion whipping smaller fish to and fro on its turbulent current.

"There are an awful lot of wrecked ships down there." Cody pressed his forehead against the tube.

"What do you think these tubes were made for?" Catherine asked.

Matt readjusted so he could put his arm around her and pull her closer. He needed human contact. Not just any human, but Catherine. Having her next to him, even in the heat radiating from the stone column so near to them, was the only thing keeping him together. The only thing keeping him from losing it as his mind wandered to thoughts of Darin being ripped apart by those demonic insects. Eaten alive. He shuddered.

"Matt?" Catherine whispered. "Don't think about it right now. Think about my question. The mystery."

She knew. Of course she knew where his mind kept taking him. He kissed the top of her head and thought about her question for a few seconds. "Maintenance. I bet the tubes are for maintenance of the wires."

She nodded, running her hand up and down his arm. "I bet you're right. That makes sense."

"So what's the plan, man?" Justin asked. "I can't just sit here." He rubbed his face like it was crawling with lice. "I need to keep moving."

Matt shrugged, no longer willing to be the decision maker.

"Let's keep going down," Cody suggested. "I'd like to see what else is swimming around down here. Plus it's going to be a while before it'll be safe for us to surface again."

Stacy stared forlornly out into the murky water. "It will never be safe for us."

"C'mon, let's keep moving." Cody scooted down the tube, disappearing from sight as it curved around the rock column.

The others followed him, Matt and Catherine bringing up the rear.

As they rounded the curve, Catherine bumped into Justin. "Hold still," he whispered.

"Why? What's . . ." Catherine clutched Matt's arm.

An enormous creature glided toward them at an incredible speed.

"Not again," Matt murmured.

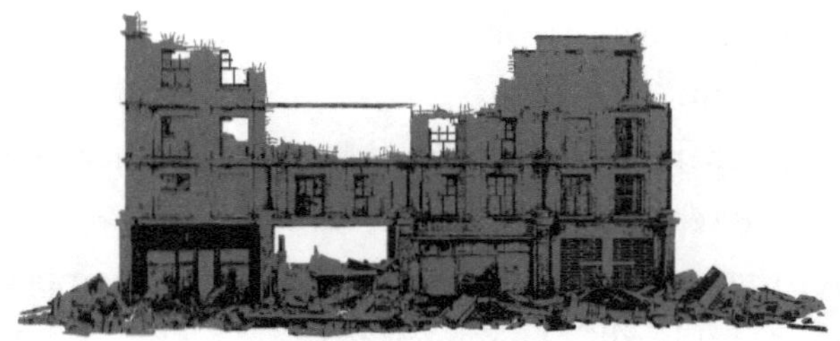

CHAPTER 31

"What is that thing? It can't get us in here, can it?" Stacy whimpered.

Cody shook his head. "Some kind of mutated alligator-sabertoothed-shark monster."

Matt stared, eyes wide, as the creature circled around the column and tube, disappearing behind them, then reappearing in seconds. Cody had summed it up almost perfectly. Its resemblance to an alligator ended with its shape, though. "Its skin is like a shark's." Matt followed the monster with his eyes. "How many eyes does it have?" He tried to count the row of eyes that started on one side of its elongated snout, ran up over it, and ended on the other side.

"Seven, I think," Catherine answered.

The monster turned away from them and swam off a distance.

"Let's get moving while that thing is over there!" Justin didn't wait for the others. He moved quickly down the tube.

"It's coming back!" Stacy shrieked.

"Justin, stop moving!" Cody shouted.

The creature spread its jaws wide—the sabertooth-like canines protruding from the top were the length of Rambo's survival knife and as thick as Matt's wrists. The tube shuddered as the creature's jaws snapped onto it. They all screamed as the monster pulled on it, jostling them back and forth.

Justin punched the wall of the tube near the creature's head and shouted, "Go away! Get the hell out of here!"

Stacy grabbed his arm and yelled, "What are you doing? Don't provoke it!"

The sabertoothed alligator shark shook its head, rattling the teens further. A crack appeared in the tube, spreading out from one of the giant canine teeth.

"Duck!" Matt yelled. The tooth pierced the tube, missing Justin by just an inch, and water flooded in through the breach. The deluge of salt water turned the pipe into a true waterslide, and they each grabbed on to the wires to keep from being flushed away.

"We have to go back up!" Matt shouted as the tube filled with water. "Go!" He pushed Catherine and Stacy ahead of him and looked frantically around for the monster as the water closed over his head.

He scrambled to catch up to the others and gulped in a breath when his head surfaced. He continued to climb, making it to where his feet were above the water. But the water kept rising. Cody lost his footing and missed as he reached for the wires. He fell, sliding past Matt like a waterslide rider. Matt's attempt to grab him failed, and his mind flashed back to Kyle—his hand slipping out of

Matt's grip, lost in the flash flood while he watched, helpless to intervene.

"Cody!" Stacy and Catherine screamed.

"I'm okay!" Cody yelled.

Matt had never been so happy to hear that Southern drawl. He looked behind him, continuing the climb up the pipe. Cody's head appeared around the curve. He dog-paddled as the churning water rose, bringing him with it. A huge weight lifted from Matt's chest. Cody was okay.

"Let's cross over," Justin said. "That tube across from us isn't filling as fast." He didn't wait for the others to concur as he pushed himself into the horizontal pipe connecting to another twisting tube.

They reached the other column and neared the ladder leading straight up through the island. Matt was last to reach the ladder, the water churning below him, rising faster than before. The monster creature torpedoed through the sea directly below Matt and slammed into the tube, biting into it and shaking its head as it tried to dislodge the tube from the column. The jar of the collision shook the teens, and they screamed as they held tight to the rungs of the ladder.

Matt, only clinging to the bottom rung with one hand, slipped and fell into the raging water. His heart pounded against his ribs, and he flailed, unsure what direction he faced. His lungs burned as he kicked his feet and flapped his arms in a panicked attempt to find which way was up—and air. His head broke the surface just long enough for him to gulp for air, only partially succeeding as the rushing water followed the air into his lungs. Black spots floated in his vision. His lungs burned and his chest felt like it was being crushed by an anaconda. He was going to die. His brain pushed against his skull. He squeezed his eyes shut against the pressure—it was going to explode.

Something latched on to his arms, his shirt. For a terrifying moment, he thought it was the creature. It pulled him upward. His friends. They pulled him onto the ladder, out of the reach of the water—and the creature. His first attempt to breathe failed as his lungs spasmed, expelling seawater all over Justin's face.

"Dude!" Justin snorted.

Matt drew in enough breath to elicit a coughing fit. Catherine pounded on his back. When the hacking subsided, Matt leaned his forehead against the rung he gripped with all his might, sucking air into his battered lungs. Again, his thoughts turned to Kyle. What he'd felt as he drowned. Matt knew now. Guilt tore through him and he sobbed, so grateful and relieved that his friends saved him, but still devastated that he wasn't able to save Kyle.

Catherine put an arm around him, holding on to the ladder with her other hand, and laid her head on his shoulder. "It's okay, Matt. You're okay."

He nodded and took a shuddering breath before lifting his head. "Thank you. All of you."

"Well, o' course, buddy." Cody slapped him on the shoulder. "Heck, you've saved all of us enough times—figured we owed you."

Matt shook his head, the emotions and guilt welling up again. He swallowed it down. "Let's get out of here."

CHAPTER 32

The climb out of the tube was silent except for the rushing water slapping against the broken tube below them. Matt's lungs burned and he coughed every time he tried to take a deep breath. He pulled himself over the lip of the tube after the others and lowered himself to the muddy ground with a grunt.

"Wow," Catherine whispered.

He looked at her, her eyes wide with wonder, then looked around and gasped. They'd emerged in a new area of the island after crossing to the other tube. "The mountain. We made it." Matt's hoarse voice sounded more like Shaggy from *Scooby Doo* than himself, but he didn't care. They'd made it to the base of the mountain.

"And no dinosaur bugs," Stacy said.

"Or underwater mutant creatures." Cody smiled.

"Yeah," Justin chimed in. "And what is it with you and water, Texas? You fell in the reservoir under the control room thing and then you fell in again today. What a dip."

"Hey!" Cody objected. "Matt fell in today too."

"Naw. He was pulled in by the water monster shaking the tube. You just fell."

Cody laughed. "I guess you're right. The shower I took yesterday just didn't get me clean enough, so I decided to seize on the opportunity to take a swim."

"Did any of our packs make it out?" Matt asked, unable to take his eyes off the mountain he'd been trying to get to since the day he awoke from cryosleep.

"Yep." Cody dropped a soaking-wet backpack to the ground. "I dropped mine when I was trying not to drown in the waterslide, but I yanked yours off your back when we pulled you out."

Matt knelt down and opened the pack, exclaiming, "Found it!" as his hand came out gripping a pair of binoculars. He put them to his eyes and looked toward the mountain. "One lens is cracked, but I can see just fine through the other one." He adjusted the focus and grinned.

"What do you see?" Catherine asked.

"Take a look for yourself." He handed her the binoculars.

"It's a huge door." She passed the binoculars to Cody. "Like a vault door—and it says B-35 on it! How far away do you think it is?"

"Maybe a mile." Matt smiled down at her, and she threw her arms around his neck and kissed him hard on the mouth.

"We're so close," she whispered.

"Umm, like, could you two *not*." Stacy turned away from them and wiped at her cheeks.

Again, guilt welled up in Matt's stomach, and he pulled away from Catherine's embrace. Seeing them together like that was probably like rubbing salt in a fresh, new wound for Stacy. He still couldn't believe they'd lost Darin—especially the way they did. He didn't think he could handle it if he lost Catherine. He looked back at her and smiled. "Hopefully today's the day you meet my parents."

"There's the rockslide from where Darin was forced to blow up the side of the mountain to fake a meteor strike," Cody said, binoculars still pressed to his face.

"Let's see." Justin took the binoculars from him.

"Poor Lance-Darin." Stacy sniffed. "I can't believe what that evil man put him through. He survived all that just to get eaten by a stupid giant bug!" She broke down in sobs and Catherine wrapped her up in a hug.

"Yeah." Justin sighed. "I was just starting to like him too."

"I know it won't make missing Darin any better, Stacy," Catherine said, "but maybe you'll get to see your family today."

Stacy sniffed and lifted her head from Catherine's shoulder. "That would be bitchin'."

"Let's get going!" Matt's initial excitement returned.

A meteor streaked across the sky and slammed into the side of the mountain. Chunks of rock and ash flew from the impact, and dust and smaller rocks pelted the group. They dived for cover behind the pipe they'd just crawled from.

"Shit!" Justin spit dirt from his mouth.

"We need to hurry and get there." Matt's heart

pumped at triple speed. "We need to make sure they're all okay, our families and everyone else."

"And we need to get somewhere safer," Cody added.

As soon as the falling debris subsided, Matt motioned to the group and grabbed his backpack from where he'd left it on the ground. "Let's go!" He ran up a single-lane road and stopped after turning a corner around a clump of trees.

"Why'd you stop?" Catherine asked, coming to a halt beside him. "Oh."

Justin, Cody, and Stacy joined them, all staring at a group of dump trucks and pickups parked askew. Matt walked closer, examining burn marks, broken windows, and dents on the nearest dump truck. He laid his hand on the winch affixed to the front guard and gazed down at the attached cable on the ground, unraveled several yards in front of the truck.

"Whoever was camping out here must have left in a big hurry," Cody said. He walked slowly in the vegetation at the side of the road, winding around broken-down army vehicles and abandoned tents that had definitely seen better days. He kicked the tall grasses aside. "They appear to have left everything right where it was. O2 tanks. There's at least five fifty-gallon barrels tipped over out here—looks like they had gas or oil in them."

Matt pointed out some newer-looking tire tracks skirting around a rockslide area. "This must be where Westbrook drove to get out of the vault."

"All this equipment, the trucks and everything, has Demo Trench symbols on it." Catherine ran her fingers over a symbol plastered to the side of a dump truck.

Matt studied the image on the pickup he'd walked back over to. He recognized it from some of the manuals back at the control center. Two parallel lines with a sphere in the lower third. A single slanted line on the right side of the double lines.

Something whizzed past Matt's head and slammed into the side of the vehicle. He glanced up, then covered his head with his arms as fireballs and ice chunks flew at him from the dark gray clouds above. "Take shelter!" He ripped the door open and jumped into the cab of the truck as hellfire rained down all around.

CHAPTER 33

Justin dived in the other side and slammed the door.

"Where are the others?" Matt twisted back and forth on the seat, frantic to find Catherine. She waved from the cab of the dump truck, where Cody and Stacy hovered on each side of her. Matt blew out a breath. "They're safe."

Large chunks of hail fell amongst frozen snowballs that must have been full of methane or some other flammable gas that caused flames to engulf them as they plummeted to the ground. As Matt stared at one such ball of ice and fire as it sizzled out on the hood of the truck, the island quaked. He tried to steady himself by grabbing the dashboard and the seat back, but the tremor rocked the truck back and forth, up and down, slamming him and Justin into each other.

A fissure opened up in the ground between the pickup and the dump truck. As it expanded rapidly, the trucks slid toward the widening crevasse. Matt and Justin scrambled out of the pickup just before it disappeared and ran to more solid ground. Matt skidded to a stop and turned back toward the unfolding disaster, panic rising in his throat, choking him as he tried to draw in a breath.

Cody and Stacy appeared to be a safe distance away, but Catherine was still inside the tipping dump truck, climbing almost vertically across the seat. The door Cody and Stacy had exited from slammed shut with the shifting of the truck, and Catherine struggled to open it against gravity.

Matt's feet froze to the ground as he watched, his mind numb with terror.

With a guttural scream, Catherine forced the door open enough to slide out and jump to the ground. She ran toward Cody and Stacy as the dump truck tipped over the edge of the newly formed precipice. Matt felt a split second of relief before his eyes caught on the unspooled cable still attached to the winch of the falling truck. The cable whipped around Catherine's leg and pulled her. She fell to the ground, face first. Cody dove for her as she slid toward the widening hole. Catherine futilely pawed at the ground, desperate to find purchase.

"No!" Stacy pushed her hands against her ears and squeezed her eyes shut. "No, no, no!"

The cable tightened more. Catherine smiled at Matt. He knew her fate. She knew her fate. Everything slowed around him and his ears rang. He had the urge to puke but didn't. Catherine reached out to him as the cable became taut. Matt moved to her, but she plummeted over the edge of the chasm before he could reach her.

A split second later, everything sped up again. The sound of rocks and metal smashing emerged from the maw that swallowed Catherine. Dust formed a mushroom cloud above the crevasse. He didn't know where anyone was. He only wanted Catherine. He fought the urge to dive into the fissure to save her, to be with her.

In an instant of pure insanity, Matt ran, his mind engulfed in horror, blinding him. Justin ran beside him and pulled him to a stop just inches away from the edge. Cody and Stacy reached his side as he peered over into the chasm. The dump truck was wedged into the crack, front side facing up. Catherine lay on the grille with the heavy cable piled on top of her, one of her legs twisted at an unnatural angle.

"Catherine!" Matt yelled. Was she breathing? She was unconscious. He dropped his backpack and continued to yell down to her as he pulled the rope out.

Stacy, Justin, and Cody joined him, yelling, "Catherine! Wake up!"

Her eyes fluttered and she moaned. She rolled to her back with a grimace, then smiled up at them. She looked around her. The side of her head was plastered with blood, and she cried out as she tried to move her twisted leg. The truck dropped a foot, wedging itself even more.

"Ah!" Catherine screamed.

Matt swung the rope and threw it down to her, his heart trying to claw its way out of his chest. Catherine rolled to her side to grab the lifeline. She caught it, but the movement was too much. The dump truck dislodged, disappearing into the abyss, taking Catherine with it.

The line snapped taut, nearly taking Matt over the edge with it, but he held true.

"Help me!" He dug in his heels.

Cody and Justin stood behind him, pulling. Stacy peered over the edge.

"Can you see her?" Matt asked.

And then the line went slack. He fell backward in a heap onto Cody and Justin.

"No!" Matt screamed. He crawled to the edge once more. Nothing but dark and dust. He pounded the dirt and let out another guttural scream as he arched his back to the sky, throwing fistfuls of dirt into the air. Tears poured from his eyes and he screamed again. "Catherine! No!" He couldn't breathe. His face was a mess of dirt and never-ending tears; his chest tightened like a vise around his lungs. He sobbed, saying her name over and over, as he mechanically pulled the rope up.

The island shook again. Matt barely registered the movement or the danger it posed. Justin and Cody each grabbed him by an arm and dragged him to his feet. They led him at a run toward the vault door.

CHAPTER 34

The clouds grew even darker as Matt's friends half-dragged him toward the vault. He stumbled multiple times and would have fallen on his face if he hadn't been held up by Cody and Justin. The world was a blur, and his body wasn't performing as it should. It just wanted to shut down. *He* just wanted to shut down. Everything was numb except his heart—the part he wished would go numb the most.

Stacy reached the door first, pounded on the center of the "B-35" stenciled there, then turned back to the boys. "How do we open it? Darin would have known." The whites of her panicked-looking eyes shone through the storm's darkness.

Another barrage of fire-hail pelted the ground around them, this time accompanied by lightning. The four of them scattered, ducking for cover wherever they could find it. The rumbling thunder moved farther away, and the fire-and-ice balls grew smaller and less numerous.

Matt rubbed his face, shook his head, and set his jaw. Heartbroken though he was, he needed to find his parents. He got up and approached the door, searching it for any latches or openings. Of course it would have to be difficult—no doorknob to twist or doorbell to ring.

"Could that be the way to open it?" Cody asked from beside him, causing Matt to jump at the sound of his voice. He'd forgotten anyone else existed at the moment.

Matt examined the area Cody pointed to while Stacy and Justin leaned in for a look. A circular depression about ten inches in diameter was sunk into the thick metal door. Inside the circle was another depression, this one in the shape of a triangle about the size of his fist.

A lone sphere of hail fire shot down next to Matt, and he jumped to the side to avoid it. *Clank.* He looked down to where his feet had landed on something hard.

Kneeling, Matt brushed the dirt, mud, and ash off to reveal a large, trunk-sized metal box. The dented lid had a Demo Trench symbol emblazoned on it. Matt found the lip of the lid with his fingertips and pulled up on it. It didn't budge. He stood, crouching down to hold on to it, and used the strength of his legs to try to pry it open. He growled. "Someone find something to pry this open with. Maybe it's a way to get in, like a trapdoor to a tunnel under the vault door or something."

Cody and Justin went in different directions to search for something to use as a pry bar, while Stacy stood and stared up at the mountain before them. Matt tried again to force the box open, but ended up slumping to his butt with a grunt, hitting the ground hard and not caring. He folded his arms across his bent knees and hid his face in them. He tried to think of anything but what had just happened to Catherine—but his shocked mind wasn't in the mood to cooperate. Like flipping through a photo album, recent images of Catherine flashed one after another. Her Hulk-like strength when she forced the heavy door of the dump truck open. Her determined face as she ran for safety. The cable wrapping around her leg, pulling her to the ground, then into the pit, like a Kraken from the depths of hell.

Matt shook his head violently within the confines of his folded arms, squeezing his eyes shut against the non-stop images playing out in his head. But they wouldn't stop. Catherine, lying lifeless on the grille of the dump truck. Her twisted leg. The blood on her head. Her dark curls spread out around her. Her smile when she regained consciousness and realized she'd survived. The flash of terror in her eyes when the truck shifted. Matt being a fraction of a second late with the rope. Renewed hope when he realized she'd be able to grab the rope. Then utter devastation as the rope went slack.

An involuntary wail ripped through his throat. Then someone was beside him, arms wrapped tight around his trembling shoulders, sobbing right along with him. Stacy's fuzzy strawberry-blonde curls tickled his neck, but he barely registered it. Matt had no idea how long they sat like that—it could have been seconds or it could have been hours. But it was long enough for his energy to be spent and his tears to dry up.

Matt slowly raised his head. Cody and Justin stood a few feet away, a crowbar in Cody's hand, silently waiting. Matt patted Stacy's arm and whispered in a raw voice, "Thank you, Stacy."

She nodded and gave his shoulder one more hug before standing and wiping her face. She tucked her hair behind her ears and held out a hand to help him up. "Come on. Let's get this thing open."

Matt nodded and took her offered hand, careful not to pull his petite friend over as he stood.

Cody stepped forward and handed the crowbar to him with a sad smile. "Found it over by the fifty-gallon barrels."

"Perfect." Matt positioned the hooked end of the bar under the lip of the metal lid, wiped his face on his shoulder, then pried the lid up with a screech of rusted hinges. He dropped the pry bar to the ground and bent down to look inside the box.

"What's in there?" Justin asked, moving to stand beside him.

"It's some kind of tool." Matt lifted it out with both hands. "Or maybe a weapon." He raised the red-colored device to his shoulder, fitting it there like the butt of a shotgun. A cord trailed from just behind the "trigger" down into the metal box.

"I ain't never seen a gun or tool like that before," Cody said.

"Me either," Matt agreed. "Must be custom built." He moved it away from his shoulder and held it in front of him with both hands.

"Custom built for what?" Justin examined the tip. "Looks like a jackhammer or a drill."

"Umm, boys?" Stacy sidled over to Justin. "Notice anything about the tip of this thing?"

CHAPTER 35

Matt examined the end Stacy referred to. It reminded him of a drill bit, but not in a shape he'd ever seen before. A triangle drill bit. He snapped his head up and looked at the vault door. "A triangle drill bit." He side-stepped to better align the tool with the depressions in the door, dragging the cord with him.

Justin eyed the cord, following it into the metal box. "Pull the trigger thing. See if it even works before trying it in the door."

The drill vibrated in Matt's hands when he pulled back on the trigger, and the triangle-shaped drill bit spun counterclockwise. "It must be using the volcanic power from below the island for its energy."

Stacy sighed and rolled her eyes. "Who cares, you nerds? Just shove it in that keyhole and, like, get the door open before something else tries to burn, eat, or kill us."

Anger flashed in Matt's gut, quickly replaced with equal parts guilt and fear. Stacy was right. He nodded and attempted to fit the drill bit into the triangle keyhole.

It clanked against the metal, refusing to go in. "Help me get the trajectory right. It's freakin' hard with the length of this thing."

Cody grabbed the drill near the tip and guided it toward the matching keyhole. After a couple of adjustments, it clicked in with a solid fit. "You're all set, boss."

Gripping the gun-like drill with both hands, Matt pulled the trigger. The drill, the triangle, and the inside of the circle in which it resided turned slowly. Matt leaned into it, using his body weight and shoulder to keep the thing in place and to keep it from spinning in his hands. Sweat broke out on his forehead. "Could use a little help here," he grunted.

Cody and Justin grabbed on and helped him hold it in place. The lock stopped with a jolt, and Matt released the trigger before they all lost their grip or the drill broke. Stacy stood behind them, looking up at the mountain again, in the direction of the man-made rockslide.

Matt wiped the sweat off his face and took a couple of deep breaths. He looked at Justin and Cody. "Ready?"

They nodded, and he leaned in and pulled the trigger. The lock moved another quarter of a turn, then seized up again. Matt stopped the drill, wiped his hands on his pants, got a better grip, then nodded to his friends and pulled the trigger again. It turned a little more. The sound of gears grinding and metal popping caused a spike in Matt's adrenaline. He released the trigger and pulled the drill out of the lock and out of Justin's and Cody's hands. He looked side to side, turned in a circle to take in his surroundings with eyes darting around like hummingbirds, then looked up at the sky—fully expecting to see a catastrophic event bearing down on them. Nothing happened. In fact, the sky was clearer than it had been all day.

Matt turned to his friends. They all seemed to have experienced similar symptoms of PTSD, staring back at him with wide eyes, their faces a shade paler than a moment before.

"It was just the door," Cody said. "We aren't in the HZRD zone anymore."

"No." Stacy chewed on her dirty fingernails. "But we're still in danger. Like, get on with it!"

Shaky hands made it even more difficult than before to fit the drill bit into the triangle lock. Justin and Cody helped guide it back in, and the three boys braced themselves before Matt pulled the trigger.

The lock turned at a snail's pace, but Matt was encouraged—it felt different this time. With each degree of movement, the mechanism inside the door clicked. The lock was disengaging bit by bit. Matt tilted his head back and closed his eyes. "Come on already, just open," he said through gritted teeth.

Almost a full minute later, and likely after taking years off Matt's life, the final click sounded, and he removed the drill from the lock as the door slowly slid open.

A rush of stale air blew by them, the stench of death riding its currents. Matt's stomach heaved. The four teens looked at each other, color draining from their faces.

Stacy shook her head, her mess of curls whipping about her face in furious denial. "I can't look. I can't . . . I can't go in there."

Matt couldn't blame her. What if they were all dead? That odor . . . it could be nothing else. He pulled the neck of his T-shirt over his nose and mouth and, fighting the dread welling up inside him, he trudged through the doorway.

CHAPTER 36

Rows of bodies lined the way inside, the dead leading him down to the unknown hell they had just entered. Matt's legs were first to surrender, first to declare that it was all too much and he was done. His knees gave and he sank to the floor of the cavern.

"Hey, buddy." Cody's soft voice sounded distant, worlds away. "I know this looks bad, but they're all covered. Someone had to do that for them."

Matt blinked, some of the fuzziness leaving his sight. He looked at the bodies on each side of him. Cody was right. They'd been laid in neat rows, each one covered with a plastic tarp or a wool army blanket. *Someone* was alive. Probably more than one person. The bodies had to be moved here and covered by someone.

"Yeah . . . yeah, you're right. We need to keep going." Matt stood and looked behind Cody. "Where are Justin and Stacy?"

Cody hooked a thumb toward the vault door. "Justin's trying to get Stacy to come inside."

"Pick her up and carry her, Justin!" Matt yelled. "I need to get out of here."

"Okay, chief!" Justin sounded all too eager to do this bit of Matt's bidding.

"Oh no, you don't!" Stacy's voice rose on the last word and ended with a loud grunt of expelled air.

At any other time before, Matt would have laughed at the sight of Stacy slung over Justin's broad shoulder, her fists pounding into his back, his grin spread wide as he clamped his arms around her struggling legs. But not now. Maybe not ever again. A flash image of Catherine falling into the dark chasm slammed into him, choking off his air. Nope. He probably wouldn't ever laugh again. He rubbed his eyes with the heels of his hands, pressing hard enough to render him blind for a few seconds afterward.

"C'mon," Cody urged. "There's a door in the rock wall up ahead. Let's head for that."

Matt nodded, and they trudged toward it. He looked back to make sure Justin followed them. Stacy had stopped struggling. She hung limply over Justin's shoulder, with her hands clamped over her eyes and nose.

Cody reached the wide door first and opened it without a problem. They stepped into the warehouse inside the cavern. Matt trailed his fingers along the side of the bus they'd come in on so many years ago as he slowly walked down its length. The overhead lights flickered. Matt pulled his hand away from the bus, his fingers covered in dust. He looked around him. Everything in there was covered in dust.

At some point since entering the warehouse, Justin

had set Stacy back on her own feet. One of them had shut the door out to where the dead lay, decaying in their eternal slumber.

"I remember this place," Justin said. "I woke up as the bus was pulling in here."

"Me too." Matt pointed at a large industrial-strength double door. "That's where they took us to put us in the cryopods."

He looked each of his remaining friends in the eye, took a deep breath, and twisted the handle on the big door. It turned easily, and Matt swung the door open.

A short, blond-haired man rushed toward them.

CHAPTER 37

A group of people, both adults and children, gathered around them as they stepped through the door. The blond man reached them first and eyed them a bit warily, mouth turned down into a slight frown. "Who are you? Where'd you come from?"

"I'm Matt Voorhees. This is Cody, Justin, and Stacy." He pointed to each of them. "We came from this vault. Westbrook, the guy in charge of taking care of everything here, took us out, in our pods." Matt shook his head. "Look, it's a long story, and we've had a long and terrible day. We've been looking for this vault,"—he glanced around at the gathering crowd—"for you all, pretty much ever since we woke up."

A kind-faced woman gave the blond man a narrow-eyed look, then smiled at Matt. "I'm Suzanne. We're so glad you made it back. Come in. Have a seat. We'll get you something to eat and drink."

She led them to a seating area, but none of them sat at first. Matt searched the crowd of people for a familiar face. They all wore the same Save the Population Project uniforms—tan tank tops and tan shorts, a number over the left breast that corresponded to the number on the pod they'd been in. Not seeing his mom or dad in the group, Matt's eyes flicked to the columns. Row upon row of occupied cryopods as far as he could see into the vault.

A wall full of windows faced the columns. The opposite wall was full of small control panels, many of them with blinking lights. Multiple computers were set up haphazardly on one desk. Cody nudged him with his shoulder and pointed to a room. A bed and a cluttered desk were the only furnishings in it. "That must have been Westbrook's sleeping quarters," Cody whispered.

"Yes," Suzanne answered. She glanced at the four filthy, bedraggled teens and pursed her lips. "Is he . . . is Westbrook . . . with you?"

"No," Stacy said sharply. "He's dead. Thankfully."

Suzanne raised an eyebrow.

Matt was surprised that no one in the group seemed to be too surprised at her words. "He . . . uhh . . . he died right at the outset when a bunch of our pods fell on top of him."

Suzanne sighed. "Not to speak ill of the dead, but I'm afraid, from the looks of some of his journal entries, he'd gone rather loopy over the last decade. Plus, he recorded himself a bunch." She pointed to a toppled pile of black plastic VHS tapes. "All of those are him recording something about saving humanity and being the savior of the human race. He was trying to get everyone out to some place called HZRD, and then he was going to wake everyone up and immediately put himself in charge of saving the world from all of the disasters."

Matt nodded, and Suzanne turned to him. "Do you know of this HZRD place?" she asked.

"Oh yeah," Justin said. "And you don't want to go there."

"I can tell you all about it sometime," Matt said. "But we can tell you Westbrook was nuts. Grade A certifiably crazy."

"We are lucky to be alive." Stacy bowed her head and tried to hold back tears. Matt put his arm around her.

"Do you guys have a radio?" Matt asked. "There's some other vaults, and we could call to them. Maybe they have a lead scientist like Westbrook who could help."

A man pulled a box from below Westbrook's desk. Matt's shoulders slumped at the sight. The box was full of radio parts, clearly smashed by someone.

"He must've destroyed it before he left," he said. "We couldn't call out to anyone."

Matt had his answer. Broken radio, no emergency call. These people couldn't call out. They were stuck. No one came for them besides the four teens who were there now.

"Well, that sucks," Matt said.

"I kept the parts," the man continued, "just in case someone can jerry-rig it back together."

A little girl no older than ten brought each of the four newcomers a can of soda and some dehydrated apple slices. They sat in the uncomfortable folding chairs nearest them and nibbled on the fruit.

"How are all y'all out of your pods?" Cody asked, popping the top of his soda.

Suzanne and most of the others moved chairs around to face the teens in an informal semicircle. "Well, Westbrook woke Dave and me up just before he left in a truck loaded down with your cryopods." She nodded toward a tall man wearing eyeglasses whom Matt assumed was Dave. "He gave us a thirty-second tutorial—after we finished vomiting—about how to keep the columns from failing, told us to stay inside until he got back, and left."

"Yes," Dave said, pushing his glasses back up the bridge of his nose. "It was a highly stressful situation to leave us in. Alarms blaring. Lights blinking." He shook his head. "I was terrified we were going to lose everyone."

"But ya didn't." A man with a deeper Southern accent than Cody slapped him on the back. "Ya did a real fine job, Dave."

Dave blushed, but a small smile peaked at the corner of his mouth. "Thanks, Robby. I could not have done it without Suzanne."

"We figured things out as best as we could," Suzanne said. "We decided on day two to wake up a few more people to help, but we knew we couldn't wake everyone up because we have such limited resources."

Looking down at his hands, Dave spoke with a solemn voice. "We were not able to keep all of the cryogenic pods going, though." He removed his glasses and wiped them with the hem of his tank top before putting them back on. "Power had been lost to parts of some of the columns before Dr. Westbrook even woke us up."

The blond man, Eric, who had rushed up to them at the door said, "You saw the dead, I'm sure. You'd a had to come through there to get to the warehouse."

Matt nodded.

"We didn't know what else to do with 'em. We didn't dare go outside, because of Westbrook's warning *and* because he didn't return. We had no idea what was out there. I mean, we thought maybe he just erupted into a pile of ash as soon as he pulled out into the apocalypse." He shrugged. "So we designated the cavern area as a sort of crypt, and we piled them all up there, covered 'em up."

A tall, skinny man and a thin woman whose head came to his shoulder hurried up from one of the rows of columns. They held hands and wore hopeful smiles. Their smiles faded a little more as their gazes slipped from Matt to Cody to Stacy, and finally to Justin.

"I-i-is Nathan with you?" the man asked. "Nathan Moore?"

Matt dropped his hand to his lap, still holding a slice of dried apple, no longer hungry. He twisted the soda can around on top of his thigh as he dropped his gaze, hoping one of the others would answer. But after a prolonged awkward silence, Matt met the couple's eyes, already void of the hope he'd seen in them as they'd rushed up. They already knew by his reaction. He just needed to say the words. Matt cleared his inflamed throat, then swallowed a sudden well of emotion. Nathan had seemed like a really great kid. "He, umm, he didn't make it. I'm so sorry." Not knowing what else to say, he added, "Nathan was a good friend."

The woman, Nathan's mom, nodded and touched

Matt's arm. "Thank you. He was a good boy." She buried her face in her husband's chest and sobbed quietly. The tall man with Nathan's build and eye color hugged her close as silent tears rolled down his cheeks.

CHAPTER 38

The grieving couple excused themselves, and as Matt watched them walk away, he realized he hadn't even looked for his parents yet. He'd been inside the cryovault for at least ten minutes. He'd been so obsessed with finding them since the minute he woke up. He shook his head. His traumatized brain wasn't functioning at full capacity.

"Hey . . ." He paused, suddenly afraid to learn the answer. "Do any of you know my parents? Or know where they are? Dan and Pat Voorhees?"

The adults in the room looked at each other and shook their heads.

"They for sure aren't among those of us who are awake," Suzanne said.

But that didn't mean anything, did it? They could just be in their columns. Anxiety welled up, flooding Matt's entire being. The few apple chips he had eaten churned in his stomach. He dropped the remaining chips to the floor and set the soda down with a shaky hand. He bent at the waist, putting his head between his knees to keep from spewing everywhere.

The nausea was going to win. Matt panted, his breath coming in short, shallow gasps. His lips tingled.

"Hey, I'm, like, really good at computer stuff. Which one should I use?" Stacy's voice declared her annoyance. "Or, like, a list of where everyone is?"

Matt assumed the hand on his back belonged to Stacy, since she was sitting right next to him. It reminded him of when his mom had taught him how to Matt-itate. He counted slowly in his head, matching his breathing to the cadence.

Dave answered Stacy. "There is a computer. It's in Westbrook's sleeping quarters over there. I've had to use it from time to time to check on things. Do you know how to use it?"

Stacy nodded, standing abruptly. "Come on, Matthew." She pulled on his arm. "Quit hyperventilating, and let's go find our families."

"It's *Matt*," he mumbled. He took two more measured breaths and slowly raised his head.

Stacy pulled on him again. Cody and Justin stood. As soon as Matt was confident he wasn't going to vomit, he stood and followed his friends into the monster's lair. Stacy powered up the Apple II taking up a good chunk of the messy desk as Cody flipped through a pile of floppy disks.

"Here, try this one." Cody handed the square disk to Stacy. "It says 'Column Schematics.'"

She popped it into the slit on the front of the computer and it whirred to life. Stacy hit a few keys and

arrow buttons. Matt watched the screen go from showing numbered rows and columns to a list of names.

"Voorhees," Stacy whispered as she scrolled down the
long, alphabetized list. "You *would* have a name that's at
the end of the alphabet."

"There!" Matt pointed as he spotted his and his parents' names on the list. "Pod locations forty-two twelve
six and forty-two fifteen nine." He scribbled the numbers
on a notepad. "Go back to the schematics."

Stacy sighed. "Fine. But then I'm going to find my
own family."

"And ours," Justin said, pointing to himself, then
Cody.

Keys clicked as Stacy's fingers flew over them, and
soon the diagram of pod locations flashed onto the
screen. Matt studied it for a few minutes. "Okay. I think
I get it. The first number is the column that corresponds
with age, the second number is the row top to bottom,
and the third number must be the pod's position in the
column front to back."

Justin scratched his head as he studied the blue-
print-like diagram. "I thought there were, like, five thousand people-cicles in here. How many rows and columns
are there?"

Matt pointed to a legend in the corner of the screen.
"There are twenty rows with twenty-five columns per
row."

"That just don't seem to add up to five thousand
people to me," Justin said, shaking his head.

"Like, do the math, Justin," Stacy said. "Twenty rows

times twenty-five columns equals five hundred columns; ten pods per column equals five thousand pods."

Matt was impressed with her quick calculations. He'd underestimated Stacy's intelligence too many times. The whole "valley girl" act was deceiving. He ripped the paper from the Garfield-shaped notepad he'd written on and headed out of the little room to go find his parents.

He walked along the rows, looking down at the floor, where the numbers were stenciled onto the cement.

"Whatcha doin'?" a tiny voice asked.

A young boy looked up at him as he answered, "I'm looking for my parents."

"Cool. Can I come with you?"

Matt looked around for an adult or someone that might be supervising this kid. "Umm . . . I guess so."

"Cool. I'm Jake." The kid turned back to face the open area where the chairs were and yelled, "Hey, Mom! I'm goin' with this guy to find his parents!"

Suzanne looked up and smiled at the boy, then walked toward them. "How about I come, too, Jakey? To make sure you stay out of Matt's way."

Matt nodded his appreciation to her. His nerves were already raw and functioning just below panic mode. He didn't need to be responsible for a kid right now.

The odd trio walked to column forty-two. His parents' age. Matt took in a deep breath and headed down the row, again looking at the floor where numbers were stenciled in front of the fifty-foot-tall columns. He stopped in front of the number twelve and looked up at the pods stacked on the shelves of the column. Squinting, he counted to pod six. That should be where his mom was. "Is there a ladder somewhere?" he asked without looking away.

Suzanne gestured to the side of the column, where a ladder was built into it. Matt wasted no more time as he started his climb to reach the sixth pod. He glanced over toward where his dad should be, three columns up, and noticed that a bunch of the pods in that direction were cracked open and didn't appear to have anyone in them. His heart sunk and he clung to the ladder, taking shallow breaths, as his mind wandered to what that could mean. "Come on, Matt," he whispered to himself. "Mom first."

He finished his twenty-five-foot or so climb up to the sixth pod, squeezed his eyes shut for a minute, then looked into the clear cover—his mom, a peaceful look on her face as she slept in suspended animation. She was alive.

CHAPTER 39

A few more people had joined Suzanne and Jake at the bottom of the ladder. Suzanne looked at Matt with a raised eyebrow as he stepped off the bottom rung.

"She's alive," he said, as some of the tension released from around his chest.

Suzanne gave him a quick hug. "I'm so glad."

"My dad should be up and over here." Matt walked to the base of row fifteen. The lower pods were intact and doing their jobs at keeping the occupants alive. It gave him some hope as he climbed the ladder, yet his heart still pounded out of control. The fifth pod up was cracked open. And the sixth. He hurried past the next two pods to reach his dad's, the ninth one. He wasn't there. His pod was empty.

Matt looked down at the group of people below him. "What does it mean if the pod is open and he isn't in it?"

A couple of the people far below just bowed their heads. Suzanne shook hers.

His dad was dead. That's what it meant.

Devastation crashed into him. His knees gave, and he almost lost his hold on the ladder—and he didn't even care in that moment. A forty-foot plunge to the cement might be a blessing. But as the tears came flooding out of his eyes, he remembered his mom. He wrapped his arm around a rung of the ladder and held tight as he sobbed, not caring who heard his cries.

The weight of everything that had happened since a frantic Cody had freed him from his cryopod by smashing the cover with a tree branch came crashing down on him. All the death. His friends. Catherine. All his fault. Even this one, his dad's death. If he'd only gotten here sooner, maybe . . . He slammed a fist into the empty pod, barely registering the sharp pain that shot through his hand.

Matt cried himself to exhaustion. He had no idea how long he'd been up on that ladder next to the pod where his dad had died. Long enough that his muscles ached and felt as weak as a newborn kitten's. His tears had all dried up, but his throat still hitched every few breaths as he continued to press his forehead against a rung.

The ladder vibrated as someone climbed it beneath him. Matt didn't even look to see who it was. After a few minutes, a hand gripped the side next to him and the person touched him on the back.

"Matt, buddy." Cody's voice was soft, for his ears only. "I'm so sorry about your dad." He let that hang there for a couple of minutes, his hand still pressed against Matt's back in support.

Finally, Matt responded, still not lifting his head. "Thanks. If I could have gotten here sooner—"

"No way I'm gonna let y'all blame yourself. You heard 'em say that some of the people were dead before Westbrook even woke Suzanne and Dave. And heck, ain't no one who tried harder to get here than you. You ain't responsible for this whacked-out place or all the crazy things out there hell-bent on killin' us, Matt. The way I see it, we're all just lucky to be alive."

Matt didn't think "lucky" was a word that fit this situation. But maybe Cody was right about it not being his fault. Westbrook had done this. He murdered Matt's dad. For what? To stroke his own hubris? What about all the others? Jim Westbrook was a mass murderer!

He sighed and lifted his head away from the ladder, swaying a little as a wave of dizziness swept over him. Cody's strong arm tightened across his back as his hand locked on to the other side of the ladder. His friend's support warmed Matt's heart a little.

"Y'all okay?" Cody asked.

Nodding, Matt replied, "Yeah. Just a little dizzy."

"I reckon we should be climbing back down soon before Stacy and Justin decide to come up here and rescue us. You ready?"

"Yeah." Matt tested his strength by bending his knees one at a time while standing in place on the ladder. "But maybe you ought to stick close to me, just in case. I think my body has had enough and might just decide to fail me at any moment."

"I've got ya, buddy."

"I know." Matt realized in that moment that he did know. And that was reason enough to toughen up and keep going.

They made it to the bottom, where Matt realized most, if not all, of the vault's conscious inhabitants had gathered.

Stacy grabbed him around the waist in a fierce hug. "I'm sorry, Matt," she whispered.

He hugged her back. He and Stacy had their differences, but she really was a good friend. He pulled away, realizing that in his grief, he hadn't even asked his friends about their own families. "What did you guys find out about your families?"

"We just wrote down their numbers," Justin said. He put a hand on Matt's shoulder. "We saw the commotion down here and wanted to make sure you were okay. Well, as okay as you can be in this crappy situation."

Now Matt really felt like a jerk. He'd been so pushy, so intent on finding his parents—not just today, but this whole time—he'd frequently forgotten the other kids had loved ones here too. "Well"—he looked at the three of them—"let's go find them."

CHAPTER 40

Stacy handed Matt a page from the notebook with two numbers written on it. "I found Catherine's parents' locations. I figure we should try to find all the other kids' families, too, like Kim and Rhett. But I wanted to start with Catherine."

Matt took the paper, again surprised by Stacy's thoughtfulness.

"Did you say Catherine?" A burly man he hadn't seen earlier made his way through the small crowd. "Would that be Catherine Turner?"

That's where she got her dark, curly hair from, Matt thought as he met the man's eyes. "Yes, sir. Catherine was . . . she was with us."

Matt's use of the past tense hit the man squarely in the gut.

He doubled over, hugging himself around the middle. "My little girl." It took him a few moments to regain his composure. He straightened up, wiped his face, and nodded as he looked at Matt. "What happened?"

Matt couldn't do this. Her terrified face flashed in his mind, and he closed his eyes as he spoke. "She was with us . . . She made it . . . almost made it . . ." He shook his head and turned away. He'd thought he was too tired to cry anymore. He was wrong.

Cody told Catherine's dad what happened to her, then said, "She was an amazing girl, sir. Strong and level-headed. Loyal."

"Thank you, young man. All four of you." His voice hitched. "It's probably a blessing that her mom is no longer here to feel this . . . this heartbreak. But in my selfishness, I wish she were. I wish she were here to share with me—the grief, the memories, everything."

Matt looked down at the paper in his hand, crinkling it as Catherine's dad walked away.

"Come on, guys," Suzanne said to the small group of survivors. "Let's go get some work done while these young people find their families."

Cody handed Matt a paper with a list of names and numbers written on it. "Here's all of our families. You choose where to start."

He really didn't want to do this. Exhaustion, both physical and emotional, tugged at his eyelids, begging him to go curl up in a corner and sleep for a week. But these were his friends. They'd survived together. He needed to help them. "Okay. Justin's parents are close by, so let's start there."

Justin's parents were both still asleep. As much as he'd badmouthed them, as awful as his life with them had been, relief still showed when he hugged the pods, finding them alive. Matt looked back at the paper. "That's it? No brothers or sisters?"

"That's it. Once you've been given the perfect child, no need to have any more." Justin flexed his muscles with a grin.

Stacy rolled her eyes.

The columns where Cody's parents were supposed to be were closer than Stacy's family—who were kind of spread all over—so the four of them went there next. Cody's shoulders relaxed a little to see them, still breathing in animated suspension.

Matt squeezed Cody's shoulder, then looked at Stacy. "You ready? We'll check your parents next."

"I'm ready," she answered.

Her parents remained safely frozen in their pods. They looked quite a bit older than Matt's parents, but he guessed that was to be expected since Stacy was the youngest of five kids. As they traipsed from row to row, column to column to find her four older siblings, Matt asked, "How in the world did all of you guys get picked in the lottery? I mean, parents and minor children were a package deal, but your brothers and sisters are all adults, and each of them would have had to be chosen separately . . ."

As Stacy shrugged, Justin tapped a finger on his chin sarcastically. "Hmm, I don't know . . . maybe because they're *rich* and bought their way in?"

Stacy stopped short, hands on her hips. "How dare you say that, Justin! My parents would never . . . I mean, like, they couldn't have . . . They wouldn't have been able . . ." She turned and looked at Matt. "Would they have been able to?"

"I don't know," he answered.

"Does it really matter at this point?" Cody rubbed

his face. "I mean, we're all here. We all made it. Let's go find the rest of Stacy's family. I'm ready to sit for a spell."

All four of Stacy's siblings were safely tucked away in their pods. *Some people get all the luck*, Matt thought. But he was too tired to feel bitter. He *was* happy for her. And he had to give her credit—her usual disregard for the feelings of those around her seemed to be dampened at the moment. Maybe she was still trying to decide if her parents gamed the system somehow. Or maybe she'd finally tapped into the empathy reserve she'd been hiding.

When the four teens stepped out into the open from the cryopod section, Suzanne met them. "I know you all are tired and need to clean up and get some rest, but is it okay if we just have a short, informal meeting before you do that?"

Matt looked at the others, and they all nodded. "Sure," he answered for the group.

Suzanne called the adults over, and they arranged the chairs in a circle so they could all see and hear each other.

"Well, first I want to welcome our new arrivals," Suzanne began. "Matt, Justin, Stacy, and Cody—the only survivors of the seventeen-year-olds' column."

The short, blond-haired man who'd greeted them spoke. "Yeah, welcome. We're all gonna starve, but welcome."

"Eric is our resident pessimist," Suzanne said.

Before Matt could even organize his thoughts into a response, Stacy jumped up, walked over to Eric, and stood in front of him as he wilted away from her in his chair.

CHAPTER 41

Stacy thrust her hands on her hips and raised an angry eyebrow. "Listen, jerk face! We've been through hell out there in the godforsaken apocalyptic *real* world while you've been inside this vault cowering in fear. If you're so worried about *starving*, maybe you should go out there and hunt down a few of the giant killer insects that dragged my Lance-Darin away and *ate him alive*!" She leaned closer to his face with each of her last three words, her voice rising in pitch.

Suzanne glanced at Matt, eyes a little wide. "You're right, Stacy. Eric is being insensitive." She cast Eric a scowl as Stacy whirled about and returned to her seat. "We are very happy you made your way here. And we have enough provisions to sustain us for a while."

"And we haven't even finished exploring this whole place. There could be more," Dave added.

"I agree with Miss Suzanne." Robby nodded in her direction. "Glad to have y'all here." He pointed at Cody and grinned. "Especially you, Tex. Now I ain't the only Southern boy here for them to make fun of."

Cody gave him a half-hearted smile.

"We do need to be conservative, however," Dave said, looking down at the floor. "I propose that we refrain from awakening anyone else for the time being so as to sustain the limited resources we have at this time. We can revisit this decision when we've been able to procure more food."

Eric straightened up like he was going to say something, but with a nervous glance at Stacy, he slumped back down.

"How do you kids feel about that?" Suzanne asked.

Cody, Justin, and Stacy looked at Matt to answer. He sighed, still the reluctant leader. "I agree. The good news is that we know a few places where we can get supplies, and one of those isn't too far from here. The bad news is that it'll be dangerous to get there and back."

"What kind of supplies?" Eric asked.

Matt, Cody, Justin, and Stacy took turns telling them about the hotel and the big storage building, the Sev, and the HZRD building. They outlined the dangers involved in getting to each place, and agreed with each other that the HZRD area should be considered off limits like a dangerous, condemned building, falling apart piece by enormous piece. Matt knew *he*, for one, would not be going back down into that underground death trap.

"I am relieved to hear about large stores of food nearby. We will have to work on finding a safer route back to the hotel than the one you took here," Dave said. "This seems like the safest place for us for the time being, and hopefully we can learn more about keeping the pods going and the inhabitants safe. We found a large supply of the nutritional substance being pumped through the feeding tubes, and the people in suspended animation need very little of it while their systems are sleeping—just enough to keep vital functions supported. Hopefully it will be enough to keep them safe in their cryogenic pods until the apocalypse stabilizes."

"But, like, *is* it safe here?" Stacy asked.

Dave looked at Suzanne and shrugged.

"That's a good question," Suzanne said. "I mean, I think it's safe for now. Our only threat is if we have to wake more people up when columns start to fail. We will run out of food and water."

"Yeah, but Westbrook said the vault was failing. That's why he piled our pods all up on a truck and took off," Justin said.

The adults all looked at each other, an air of confusion around them. Suzanne shook her head. "I don't know. I honestly don't know. He seemed so frantic when he woke Dave and me up. But we were both so dazed, and he rushed through his instructions to us. He spent a total of maybe five minutes telling us how to keep the pods going, then he rushed out of here, telling us he'd be back."

"Yes, Suzanne is correct," Dave added. "The pods that were inoperative at that time seem to have been that way for a while. They were not newly compromised."

Matt clenched his fists. "Darin was right about the whole thing. Westbrook was crazy and just wanted to be the savior of humanity. That's why he made Darin set off the explosion, and that's why he faked the vault failure."

Matt spent a few minutes putting the whole story together. Westbrook faking a meteor strike, making Darin explode the outside, causing the columns to fail so he could continue the lie of saving people. Placing them in the HZRD building and becoming their leader.

The adults listened intently while Matt threaded it all together. When he mentioned they were on an island, it took a little convincing, but by the end, they all agreed that Westbrook's twisted plan was the whole reason they were in this mess.

"Some savior," Justin scoffed. "His stupid scheme just ended up killing him and most of our group."

"Okay," Matt said, "so we should be reasonably safe here. What do you all know about how to keep the pods going?"

"Not much, I'm afraid," Dave said. "We've been lucky so far. I've been able to figure out what some of the alarms mean and how to stave off disaster. There aren't any instructional manuals I've been able to find around here."

Matt nodded, making up his mind. "I'll take Westbrook's place for the time being, then. I've seen how he ran this place by watching the VHS tapes he stowed in my pod. It isn't as good as an instruction manual, but it will have to do for now. I'll take care of the pods until I can teach someone else."

"Great." Suzanne clasped her hands together. "Let me show you four where the shower is and where you can get some rest."

CHAPTER 42

"This is awesome!" Jake said with a mouthful of some sort of pasta dish he'd chosen from the box of MREs Matt and Cody had brought back from their latest trip to the hotel. The young boy's lips and half of his face was slathered in the red sauce. The months had passed, and everyone was happier and healthier.

Suzanne finished chewing and swallowed before she said, "Jake, don't talk with your mouth full. And I agree." She turned to Matt. "I'm so glad Cody got that big truck running and the two of you found a safer route back to the hotel. I was really getting tired of eating dried fruit and stale nuts."

"How much food did you say is stored there?" Dave laid out each package from the MRE he'd chosen in a neat line, starting with the main course and ending with the dessert.

"A crap ton," Cody answered.

"I noticed y'all brought back some guns and ammo

this time." Robby licked gravy off his fingers. "Y'all still plannin' on trying to hunt some of those bugs?"

"Yeah," Matt said. "I think so. Even if they end up not being edible, killing them off will make this place a lot safer."

"Eww." Stacy screwed her face up in disgust. "Edible? Gag me with a spoon!"

"Whatever, Stace," Justin said. "You told me the other day that you've eaten *snails* before. Not that big of a difference, in my opinion."

"Uhh, like, escargot is a delicacy."

Suzanne laughed. "You know, people all over the world subsist on insects like grasshoppers and dragonflies, even tarantulas, during the lean months of the year."

"No thank you!" Stacy huffed. "I won't eat them, but I'll sure help you kill the evil demons."

They ate in silence for several minutes. Matt thought about how they'd all settled into a routine of sorts in the months since arriving at the vault. He'd been able to train a couple of the adults on how to take care of the cryopods and keep the people inside alive. Since finding a safer route to the hotel, they'd been able to bring back food and other supplies a couple of times.

Matt looked around the area they'd designated as the dining room. A couple of the most recently awakened people sat talking two tables over. Matt was anxious to wake his mom, but agreed with the lottery system Dave had come up with to make it fair. Every few weeks, after bringing in new supplies, a couple of the awake people were chosen in a drawing, and those people got to pick who to wake up next. Supplies weren't the only thing he'd brought from the hotel. He'd finally worked up the nerve to bring the tape recorder back. He desperately wanted to hear Catherine's voice again.

Robby and one of the newly awakened women strolled in from the warehouse. Robby wiped dirt from his hands onto his pants. Matt smiled, remembering the "yee haw!" the country-born man had hollered when Matt handed him a pair of jeans he'd brought back from the storage building at the hotel. Robby and the woman, Julie, had been working on nutrifying a large section of soil beds out in the warehouse in the hopes they would soon be able to grow some food. There were enough packets of seeds in the storage building to cover the entire island, and then some, with fruit and vegetables.

"How's it looking out there?" Matt asked.

Robby smiled at Julie, and they sat across from him. "Great! I think we'll be ready to plant our first experimental crops within the next week or two."

"What are you going to plant?" Matt was hoping for watermelon.

"We'll start with the vegetables we know are the easiest to grow," Julie said. "Carrots, green beans, squash, and tomatoes."

"No fruit?" Matt asked.

"If the veggies start growing, we'll try some fruit." Robby smiled. "Berries are pretty easy to grow, so we'll start with some strawberries, raspberries, and blueberries. How does that sound?"

Matt nodded. "Sounds great. To be honest with you, anything fresh sounds good, even green beans."

Robby laughed and gripped Matt's shoulder as he

stood. "I'm gonna go check out the MREs y'all brought back today. I'm starvin'." He looked down at Julie. "Want me to bring you something?"

She shook her head and stood. "I'll come with you. I want to see what the choices are."

Matt finished his meal and gathered up the packages. After throwing his trash in the compactor, he entered the office.

"How's it going?" he asked.

Stacy swiveled in the chair. "Great! The alarms look good and the columns are stable for the time being."

"None have failed for a while."

"I know," she said. "It's a miracle."

"You're the miracle, Stacy." Matt put a hand on her shoulder. "Without you keeping an eye on all this tech on a constant basis, we would be SOL."

"Well, thanks, Matt. I truly love it. It's like my calling in life or something like that."

"It truly is." He turned to leave.

"Hey, Matt?" Stacy said.

"Yeah."

"One of these times you go back to the hotel, can you grab that computer from the lab?"

"Absolutely!"

"It'll be super helpful to monitor the columns. You know, make sure there's no glitches in the system."

"We will pick it up for you."

Matt left the area they deemed the office and stood in front of his mom's column, staring up at her pod. He missed her and wanted so badly to be able to wake her up. He wanted to tell her about Catherine—the others, too, but mostly Catherine. Matt sighed and continued on to the last column. A couple of the columns there had been having issues. He was worried they were going to completely fail before they had enough supplies to wake them all up. None of them wanted more people to die—not from either a failing pod or from starvation.

Matt clenched his jaw; his anger at Westbrook flared anew every time he thought about the intentional damage that had been done when he'd sent a young Darin out to set off explosions so the scientist could artificially save the world. Plus, who knew what other intentional sabotage he'd pulled when Darin was in cryosleep? The breach had been fixed, and the cave itself was a good enough shelter for the time being, but the damage had been done and the columns would fail sooner or later—especially these ones. Matt climbed up the ladder in front of him, carefully checking the tubes and wires keeping the inhabitants of the pods alive in frozen sleep.

As he climbed back down, footsteps echoed down the row toward him. "I figured you'd be down here checkin' on these columns," Cody said. "How are they doin'?"

"Okay for now." Matt stepped off the last rung onto the cement floor. "What's up? Is everything okay?"

"Everything's good. The others asked me to come get ya. Dave did the math on the supplies we brought back and gave the green light to do another drawing to wake a couple more people up. They're all waitin' for you to get started."

CHAPTER 43

Lily, the ten-year-old girl who had brought Matt and his friends food and drinks their first day there, stuck the tip of her tongue out in concentration as she reached into the large tin coffee can and stirred the small slips of paper inside. The can was held aloft by Suzanne, high enough that Lily couldn't see into it.

"Come on, Lily, just pick one," an exasperated Jake whined.

With an annoyed look in Jake's direction, Lily pulled a piece of paper out of the can. She unfolded it and looked at it, then smiled over at Matt where he stood off to the side of the crowd. "Matt Voorhees!" she shouted.

"Yes!" Matt pumped a fist in the air as Cody pounded him on the back in celebration. For the first time since finding the vault, Matt felt relief. He didn't expect the tears, but they came without warning. Then sadness struck. He was waking her up, only to tell her his dad was gone. He pushed that feeling aside for now. This was his first true win since being put into cryosleep decades ago.

* * *

The built-in lift for column forty-two moved Pat Voorhees's pod horizontally until it cleared the pods below it. Dave, standing on the column's ladder next to it, unplugged the wires connecting it to the power source running through the center of the pillar. He signaled a thumbs-up down to Cody, who toggled the switch that started the pod on its slow descent to the ground.

Matt shifted his weight back and forth from one foot to the other. His stomach fluttered, and he ran his hand over the short stubble of his fresh buzz cut. The closer the pod got to the floor, the faster his heart raced—he thought he might faint. He bent at the waist, resting his sweaty palms on his knees.

Justin stepped over to him and gripped both of Matt's shoulders in his hands, squeezing just enough to hurt a little. "Relax, chief. This is what you've been wanting since day one at Camp New Beginnings. It'd be a real bummer if your mom woke up to find you sprawled on the floor, passed out like a drunk who's been on a three-day bender."

Matt nodded. Justin was right. He took a slow, deep breath, then blew it out through pursed lips. He stood up and looked Justin in the eyes. "Thanks, man. I think I'm okay now."

With one more squeeze to his shoulders, Justin gave a quick head nod and moved to stand next to Stacy.

The pod now safely on the floor, Matt stepped up to it and slipped the chain with the spare key they found in Westbrooks's effects from around his neck. A solemn memory of Catherine and how she found the key on the first day entered his mind. He grasped the key in his shaky hand and fit it into the inconspicuous lock that was flush with the plastic. With a twist of his wrist, the airtight lid hissed, and Matt lifted it, smiling down at his mom.

Her eyes fluttered open. She blinked a few times before focusing in on her son. "Matt." Her voice cracked as it adjusted to being used after decades of lying dormant. She grabbed his hands and started to sit up. "Did we make it? Is it over?"

Matt gently urged her back down, gripping her hands as tears formed in his eyes. "Mom, lie back for a minute while we get the feeding tube out."

Suzanne stepped up next to him, removed the feeding tube, placed a piece of gauze over the site, and taped it down. She laid a plastic bag on his mom's lap, gave Matt's arm a squeeze, and stepped away from the long-awaited reunion of mother and son.

Oh yeah, Matt thought. *I almost forgot.* "Mom, you're probably going to throw up." He let go of her hands and gave her the bag—just in time—as her face turned ashen and she retched into it.

When she appeared to be done, Suzanne handed her a damp washcloth and a cup of water and took the bag of vomit from her.

Matt's mom wiped her face and rinsed her mouth out, then took his hands again and smiled up at him.

"Okay, Mom," Matt said, "when you're ready, I'll help you out of this thing." He turned his head to wipe tears away on his shoulder.

"I'm ready, sweetheart."

She swung her legs over the side and Matt helped her stand. As soon as her feet hit the floor, she pulled him in for a hug that lasted several minutes. She finally pulled away just enough to look at him. "Matty, you look so good. How long have you been out? Where's your dad?" She craned her neck to look around him.

Matt took a breath; this was the moment he had been dreading. "There's a lot I need to tell you. Let's go sit down so we can talk." He didn't dare look at her face. He knew she'd see straight through to his sorrow, and he wanted to delay her grief for just a minute longer. He took her by the arm and led her out of the cryopod area to a corner of the common room, where he'd set up two chairs and had a wool blanket waiting for her.

As Pat Voorhees sat wrapped in the scratchy blanket, Matt sat across from her, knee to knee. "Mom." His guts twisted like he was just hearing the news again for the first time. "He . . . Dad . . . He didn't make it. I'm so sorry." The dam broke, and Matt's vision—his face, his throat, everything—flooded with tears. "His pod failed. He was gone when I got here . . . when I got back here." He shook his head. There was so much to tell her.

His mom lunged toward him and he opened his arms to accept her in his embrace. Matt's heart ached for her. It ached for him. Their shared grief seemed to multiply the sorrow, at least for a time. She sobbed in his arms as the tears silently slid down his face. He would be strong for her. She needed him to be strong.

"I loved your dad so much," she whispered in a quavering voice. "He was my knight in shining armor. My best friend. He was the best dad. The best husband."

Matt nodded, holding her tighter.

When her sobs subsided, she leaned into his chest for a few minutes longer before sitting back in her chair. She touched his face like she'd always done when he was younger. "You seem so much older, more mature. Tell me what you've been through."

So he told her everything.

"I'm confused." She shook her head. "This man—Westbrook—he knowingly put you in a deadly sound-stage? A made-up simulation?"

"Yes." Matt nodded. "And if he hadn't wrecked and died, you'd all be there too."

Her face twisted with anger. "No, we wouldn't. Surely we'd be dead. At least half of us. Five thousand people with few resources, deadly weather, and a madman at the helm . . . Fully grown adults don't do as well under pressure as you four did. I hate that he did this to the four of you."

"I need to fess up, Mom. Camp New Beginnings was just the tip of the iceberg." Matt's eyes filled with tears. "There were eleven of us."

"Eleven?!" Pat's voice cracked. She pulled her son into a hug, and she cried. "Seven *kids* died?"

And here it was. Matt had the macabre task of retelling each and every death in detail. He smiled and choked back tears when talking about Catherine. Her loss still stung him to his core.

"You really liked her, didn't you, Matt?"

"I did. I loved her."

Pat cocked her head to the side, and a sad smile

formed on her face. "For love to exist, utter heartbreak must, too, I'm afraid. I'm so sorry."

He'd never considered that before. "I guess that makes sense. Same as how you can't have good without evil. Westbrook was evil."

Matt continued pausing when he needed a break, and doing his Matt-itation when things were too overwhelming.

"I didn't know you still did that." Pat rested a hand on his knee. Her demeanor had softened—no longer furious with the circumstances Dr. Westbrook had put them in. "Does it still keep the scaries away?"

"Yeah!" Matt stifled a laugh. "But don't call it 'the scaries.' I'm almost eighteen—actually, I'm probably like forty years old or something in real time."

"Sorry, old man." She beamed.

"For real, Mom, I don't think I could have coped, let alone led, without it. You and Dad…"

"I know, honey, I know," she reassured him. "Tell me the rest."

Matt couldn't bring himself to look her in the eyes, and instead powered through the rest.

". . . So me, Cody, Justin, and Stacy have been going out to scavenge supplies. We've been cleaning out the hotel a little each time we go there. Even though it's only partially finished, I think it'll be a good place for some of us to stay when it gets too crowded here. And there's one more thing. Before we made our final push here, the six of us—including Darin and Catherine—made a recording. Do you want to hear it? A lot of it was what I've already told you, but I'm sure I've forgotten some things. Or we can skip to the end, and you can hear the best part."

"You pick, I trust your judgment."

Matt hesitated, then rewound until he found their final entry. Ghosts from the past, the speakers crackled to life. He knew what his friends, the six musketeers as Catherine had called them, were about to say. But still, he sat on the edge of his seat. Darin's voice haunted him, and it probably always would. He was a traumatized boy, and Matt had pushed him, maybe too hard, for the truth.

His mother stayed silent the duration of the tape until Catherine spoke.

"She had a lovely voice, Matt."

"Yeah, she did." He bit his lip. The tape finally stopped with a *click*. "Well, now you know everything. Do you have any questions?"

"Not right now. It's a lot to process," his mom said. "Matt, thank you."

"For what?"

"For waking me up. For being so brave, so grown up. For getting food for everyone and making sure the pods are safe. For everything. You amaze me."

"You're welcome, Mom. I just want you to know that my intentions are good."

EPILOGUE

The military cargo truck bounced along the terrain at a faster speed than they probably should have been going. The boombox in Justin's lap blared Bruce Springsteen's "Born in the USA." Deena, a sixteen-year-old new-comer, sang along, dancing on the seat between Matt and Justin. Matt had only been mildly surprised when Justin had won the lottery and picked the two girls to wake up instead of his parents. He'd just grinned at his friends and promised to pick his parents next time. Matt doubted it, though. Maybe this was Justin's payback for the neglect he'd endured growing up. Or maybe, he was just deeply determined to find a girlfriend. Either way, Justin seemed happier than ever.

"Maybe you should slow down a little," Brandi, also sixteen, shouted, flanked by Cody and Justin.

The five of them were crammed into the cab of the big truck, but none of them seemed to mind.

Matt reached across Deena and turned the music

down. "I can't believe how many times we drove or walked past that entrance to the HZRD this morning."

"Yeah," Justin agreed. "It was hidden in plain sight behind that outcropping of lava rocks."

"I seriously can't believe the government built that place." Brandi shook her head. "It's just crazy."

"Yeah. It's like some insane parody of *Raiders of the Lost Ark*, but without the treasure." Deena held on to the dashboard as the truck bounced over a large rut.

Matt smiled at her comparison and slowed down just a little. Maybe he and Deena had some things in common. He'd have to quiz her on her movie knowledge later.

"At least we'll be able to find it next time," Cody said. "I think we'll have the Sev cleared out with one or two more trips. This truck holds a crap ton of food and equipment."

"You guys really came all this way on foot before?" Brandi asked.

"Mostly," Justin said. "When we were underground, we traveled by tram some of the way, and we had a Wagoneer for a short time."

Matt pulled up to the vault and put the truck in Park. "How long do you think it took us to get back here today?"

"A couple of hours, maybe," Cody answered.

Matt shook his head and jumped down from the tall cab. He opened the overhead door, then got back in the truck and pulled it into the warehouse. He cranked on the wheel, turning the big truck around in the space between the partially framed-in rooms on either side of the warehouse. One of those rooms would be his and his mom's. It would be nice to have a private space for the two of them. The piles of construction material at the hotel had come in handy for this project.

Backing the truck up to the industrial garage door, Matt used the side mirrors to determine when to stop. He put the truck in Park and turned off the ignition. The five teens jumped down from the cab. He walked past the crops, which were full grown—they had been harvesting fresh vegetables for a couple of weeks now. Carrots lined rows that were sprouting mature, lacy stems off the sweet, plump orange root vegetable. It was in contrast to the nine-foot-tall soft, hairy-stemmed tomato plant. Its dark green odorous leaflets were holding on to ripe, bulbous red tomatoes.

Deena slapped his hand when he reached out to pluck a juicy red tomato from its stalk.

"You know the rules," she said.

"I know," Matt said. "I just love tomatoes. Thanks for being there in my weakness."

Deena blinked her big blue eyes and parted her lips to speak, but words didn't come out. She smiled and cocked her head to one side.

Matt cleared his throat. "Hey, have you seen *Attack of the Killer Tomatoes*?"

"That cheesy movie? I did see it."

"Yeah, it was cheesy, wasn't it?"

"I loved it!"

"Oh good. Me too." Matt's hand brushed the back of hers, and for a fleeting second, he felt complete once more.

He pounded on the inner vault door. As it slowly

opened, he flipped up the canvas shell covering the back of the truck to reveal boxes of canned food and other items filling the cargo bed.

Matt retrieved a small cardboard box and put it under his arm.

"Did you get it?" Stacy asked.

"Yup," he replied. "More floppy disks for our resident IT supervisor."

Looking over their latest haul, he said to the gathering group of people, "There's more where that came from."

Stacy playfully elbowed Matt in the ribs. "I can't believe everything that's happened since we woke up in our pods. Now here we are, figuring everything out. Makes me wonder what will happen next."

"Next? Next, we live. We live for all the people we lost. We just live."

THE END

As a kid, Tyler H. Jolley always had a knack for storytelling. When he grew bored of old fables, he created his own exciting and unique worlds. Many years later, he still had so many new ideas and stories swirling in his head, but with nowhere to share it. That's when he put his pencil to paper and let the creative juices flow.

His debut novel, *Extracted*, came out in 2013 and swiftly became an Amazon Best Seller and Spencer Hill Press Best Seller. *Prodigal* and *Riven*, the second and third books in The Lost Imperials series were released in May of 2015.

After a brief hiatus he restructured and returned to writing. His Adventurous Ali series has received much praise. To date, he's released three in the series.

When he's not writing, you can find him at his orthodontic practice, mountain biking, or on the hunt for the perfect doughnut.